W9-CBT-803

THE GREAT WAVE
And Other Stories

THE GREAT WAVE

And Other Stories

BY

MARY LAVIN

New York

THE MACMILLAN COMPANY

First Printing

The following stories originally appeared in *The New
Yorker:* "The Living" (1958); "Second-Hand," "The
Great Wave," and "The Bridal Sheets" (1959); "In
a Cafe," "Loving Memory," and "The Yellow Beret"
(1960); and were copyrighted © in the respective
years shown, by The New Yorker Magazine, Inc.

"My Molly" is reprinted by permission of *What's
New,* © 1958, Abbott Laboratories, North Chicago,
Illinois.

The author and publishers also wish to make
acknowledgment to *British Harper's Bazaar* for "The
Mouse," and Putnam & Co., Ltd. for "What's Wrong
with Aubretia?" (which appeared as "The Villas" in
Pick of Today's Short Stories, No. 10).

Printed in the United States of America

Library of Congress catalog card number: 61-12700

For
M. S.

CONTENTS

The Great Wave

THE Bishop was sitting in the stern of the boat. He was in his robes, with his black overcoat thrown across his shoulders for warmth, and over his arm he carried his vestments, turned inside out to protect them from the salt spray. The reason he was already robed was because the distance across to the island was only a few miles, and the island priest was spared the embarrassment of a long delay in his small damp sacristy.

The islanders had a visit from their Bishop only every four years at most, when he crossed over, as now, for the Confirmation ceremony, and so to have His Grace arrive thus in his robes was only their due share: a proper prolongation of episcopal pomp. In his albe and amice he would easily be picked out by the small knot of islanders who would gather on the pier the moment the boat was sighted on the tops of the waves. Yes: it was right and proper for all that the Bishop be thus attired. His Grace approved. The Bishop had a reason of his own too, as it happened, but it was a small reason, and he was hardly aware of it anywhere but in his heart.

Now, as he sat in the boat, he wrapped his white skirts tighter around him, and looked to see that the cope and chasuble were well doubled over, so that the coloured silks would not be exposed when they got away from the lee of the land and the waves broke on the sides of the currach. The cope above all must not be tarnished. That was why he stubbornly carried it across his arm: the beautiful cope that came all the way from Stansstad, in Switzerland, and was so overworked with gilt thread that it shone like cloth of gold. The orphreys, depicting

the birth and childhood of Christ, displayed the most
elaborate work that His Grace had ever seen come from
the Paramentenwerkstätte, and yet he was far from un-
familiar with the work of the Sisters there, in St. Klara.
Ever since he attained the bishopric he had commis-
sioned many beautiful vestments and altar cloths for use
throughout the diocese.   He had once, at their instigation,
broken a journey to Rome to visit them.   And when he
was there, he asked those brilliant women to explain to
him the marvel, not of their skill, but of his discernment
of it, telling them of his birth and early life as a simple
boy, on this island towards which he was now faced.

'Mind out!' he said, sharply, as one of the men from
the mainland who was pushing them out with the end of
an oar, threw the oar into the boat, scattering the air with
drops of water from its glossy blade.   'Could nothing be
done about this?' he asked, seeing water under the bottom
boards of the boat.   It was only a small sup, but it rippled
up and down with a little tide of its own, in time with the
tide outside that was already carrying them swiftly out
into the bay.

'Tch, tch, tch,' said the Bishop, for some of this water
had saturated the hem of the albe, and he set about tuck-
ing it under him upon the seat.   And then, to make
doubly sure of it, he opened the knot of his cincture and
re-tied it as tight about his middle as if it were long ago
and he was tying up a sack of spuds at the neck.   'Tch,
tch,' he repeated, but no one was unduly bothered by his
ejaculations because of his soft and mild eyes, and, didn't
they know him?   They knew that in his complicated,
episcopal life he had to contend with a lot, and it was
known that he hated to give his old housekeeper undue
thumping with her flat iron.   But there was a thing would
need to be kept dry — the crozier!

'You'd want to keep that yoke there from getting wet
though, Your Grace,' said one of the men, indicating the

crozier that had fallen on the boards. For all that they mightn't heed his little old-womanish ways, they had a proper sense of what was fitting for an episcopal appearance.

'I could hold the crozier perhaps,' said Father Kane, the Bishop's secretary, who was farther up the boat. 'I still think it would be more suitable for the children to be brought over to you on the mainland, than for you to be traipsing over here like this, and in those foreign vestments at that!'

He is thinking of the price that was paid for them, thought the Bishop, and not of their beauty or their workmanship. And yet, he reflected, Father Kane was supposed to be a highly-educated man, who would have gone on for a profession if he hadn't gone for the priesthood, and who would not have had to depend on the seminary to put the only bit of gloss on him he'd ever get — Like me — he thought! And he looked down at his beautiful vestments again. A marvel, no less, he thought, savouring again the miracle of his power to appreciate such things.

'It isn't as if *they*'ll appreciate them over there,' said Father Kane, with sudden venom, looking towards the island, a thin line of green on the horizon.

'Ah, you can never say that for certain,' said the Bishop mildly, even indifferently. 'Take me, how did I come to appreciate such things?'

But he saw the answer in the secretary's hard eyes. He thinks it was parish funds that paid for my knowledge, and diocesan funds for putting it into practice! And maybe he's right! The Bishop smiled to himself. Who knows anything at all about how we're shaped, or where we're led, or how in the end we are ever brought to our rightful haven?

'How long more till we get there?' he asked, because the island was no longer a vague green mass. Its familiar shapes were coming into focus; the great high promontory throwing its purple shade over the shallow fields by the shore, the sparse white cottages, the cheap cement pier, constantly in need of repairs. And, higher up, on a ledge of the promontory itself there was the plain cement church, its spire only standing out against the sky, bleak as a crane's neck and head.

To think the full height of the promontory was four times the height of the steeple.

The Bishop gave a great shudder. One of the rowers was talking to him.

'Sure, Your Grace ought to know all about this bay. Ah, but I suppose you forget them days altogether now!'

'Not quite, not quite,' said the Bishop, quickly. He slipped his hand inside his robes and rubbed his stomach that had begun already to roll after only a few minutes of the swell.

When he was a little lad, over there on the island, he used to think he'd run away, some day, and join the crew of one of the French fishing trawlers that were always moving backwards and forwards on the rim of the sky. He used to go to a quiet place in the shade of the Point, and settling into a crevice in the rocks, out of reach of the wind, he'd spend the day long staring at the horizon; now in the direction of Liverpool, now in the direction of the Norwegian fjords.

Yet, although he knew the trawlers went from one great port to another, and up even as far as Iceland, he did not really associate them with the sea. He never thought of them as at the mercy of it in the way the little currachs were that had made his mother a widow, and that were jottled by every wave. The trawlers used to seem out of reach of the waves, away out on the black rim of the horizon.

He had in those days a penny jotter in which he put down the day and hour a trawler passed, waiting precisely to mark it down until it passed level with the pier. He put down also other facts about it which he deduced from the small vague outline discernible at that distance. And he smiled to remember the sense of satisfaction and achievement he used to get from that old jotter, which his childish imagination allowed him to believe was a full and exhaustive report. He never thought of the long nights and the early dawns, the hours when he was in the schoolroom, or the many times he was kept in the cottage by his mother, who didn't hold with his hobby.

'Ah son, aren't you all I've got! Why wouldn't I fret about you?' she'd say to him, when he chafed under the yoke of her care.

That was the worst of being an only child, and the child of a sea widow into the bargain. God be good to her! He used to have to sneak off to his cranny in the rocks when he got her gone to the shop of a morning, or up to the chapel of an afternoon to say her beads. She was in sore dread of his even looking out to sea, it seemed! And as for going out in a currach! Hadn't she every currach-crew on the island warned against taking him out?

'Your mammy would be against me, son,' they'd say, when he'd plead with them, one after another on the shore, and they getting ready to shove their boats down the shingle and float them out on the tide.

'How will I ever get out to the trawlers if I'm not let out in the currachs?' he used to think. That was when he was a little fellow, of course, because when he got a bit older he stopped pestering them, and didn't go down near the shore at all when they were pulling out. They'd got sharp with him by then.

'We can't take any babbies out with us — a storm might come up. What would a babby like you do then?' And he couldn't blame them for their attitude because by this time he knew they could often have found a use for him out in the boats when there was a heavy catch.

'You'll never make a man of him hiding him in your petticoats,' they'd say to his mother, when they'd see him with her in the shop. And there was a special edge on the remark, because men were scarce, as could be seen anywhere on the island by the way the black frieze jackets of the men made only small patches in the big knots of women, with their flaming red petticoats.

His mother had a ready answer for them.

'And why are they scarce?' she'd cry.

'Ah, don't be bitter, Mary.'

'Well, leave me alone then. Won't he be time enough taking his life in his hands when there's more to be got for a netful of ling than there is this year!'

For the shop was always full of dried ling. When you thought to lean on the counter, it was on a long board of ling you leant. When you went to sit down on a box or a barrel it was on top of a bit of dried ling you'd be sitting. And right by the door, a greyhound bitch had dragged down a bit of ling from a hook on the wall and was chewing at it, not furtively, but to the unconcern of all, growling when it found it tough to chew, and attacking it with her back teeth and her head to one side, as she'd chew an old rind of hoof parings in the forge. The juice of it, and her own saliva mixed, was trickling out of her mouth on to the floor.

'There'll be a good price for the first mackerel,' said poor Maurya Keely, their near neighbour, whose husband was ailing, and whose son Seoineen was away in a seminary on the mainland studying to be a priest. 'The seed herring will be coming in any day now.'

'You'll have to let Jimeen out on that day if it looks to be a good catch,' she said, turning to his mother. 'We're having our currach tarred, so's to be all ready against the day.'

Everyone had sympathy with Maurya, knowing her man was nearly done, and that she was in great dread that he wouldn't be fit to go out and get their share of the new season's catch, and she counting on the money to pay for Seoineen's last year in the seminary. Seoineen wasn't only her pride, but the pride of the whole island as well, for, with the scarcity of men folk, the island hadn't given a priest to the diocese in a decade.

'And how is Seoineen? When is he coming home at all?' another woman asked, as they crowded around Maurya. 'He'll soon be facing into the straight,' they said, meaning his ordination, and thinking, as they used the expression, of the way, when Seoineen was a young fellow, he used to be the wildest lad on the island, always winning the ass-race on the shore, the first to be seen flashing into sight around the Point, and he coming up the straight, keeping the lead easily to finish at the pier-head.

'He'll be home for a last leave before the end,' said his mother, and everyone understood the apprehension she tried to keep out of her voice, but which steals into the heart of every priest's mother thinking of the staying power a man needs to reach that end. 'I'm expecting him the week after next,' she said, then suddenly her joy in the thought of having him in the home again took place over everything else.

'Ah, let's hope the mackerel will be in before then!' said several of the women at the one time, meaning there would be a jingle in everyone's pocket then, for Seoineen would have to call to every single cottage on the island, and every single cottage would want to have plenty of lemonade and shop-biscuits too, to put down before him.

Jimeen listened to this with interest and pleased antici-pation. Seoineen always took him around with him, and he got a share in all that was set down for the seminarian.

But that very evening Seoineen stepped onto the pier. There was an epidemic in the college and the seminarists that were in their last year like him were let home a whole week before their time.

'Sure, it's not for what I get to eat that I come home, Mother!' he cried, when Maurya began bewailing having no feasting for him. 'If there's anything astray with the life I've chosen it's not shortage of grub! And anyway, we won't have long to wait?' He went to the door and glanced up at the sky. 'The seed will be swimming inward tomorrow on the first tide!'

'Oh God forbid!' said Maurya. 'We don't want it that soon either, son, for our currach was only tarred this day!' and her face was torn with two worries now instead of one.

Jimeen had seen the twinkle in Seoineen's eye, and he thought he was only letting-on to know about such things, for how would he have any such knowledge at all, and he away at schools and colleges the best part of his life.

The seed was in on the first tide, though, the next day.

'Oh, they have curious ways of knowing things that you'd never expect them to know,' said Jimeen's own mother. It was taken all over the island to be a kind of prophesy.

'Ah, he was only letting-on, Mother,' said Jimeen, but he got a knock of her elbow over the ear.

'It's time you had more respect for him, son,' she said, as he ran out the door for the shore.

Already most of the island boats were pulling hard out into the bay. And the others were being pushed out as fast as they could be dragged down the shingle.

But the Keely boat was still upscutted in the dune grass under the promontory, and the tar wetly gleaming on it. The other women were clustered around Maurya, giving her consolation.

'Ah sure, maybe it's God's will,' she said. 'Wasn't himself doubled up with pain in the early hours, and it's in a heavy sleep he is this minute — I wouldn't wake him

up whether or no ! — He didn't get much sleep last night.
It was late when he got to his bed. Him and Seoineen
stayed up talking by the fire. Seoineen was explaining
to him all about the ordination, about the fasting they
have to do beforehand, and the holy oils and the chrism
and the laying-on of hands. It beat all to hear him!
The creatureen, he didn't get much sleep himself either,
but he's young and able, thank God. But I'll have to
be going back now to call him for Mass.'

'You'll find you won't need to call Seoineen,' said one
of the women. 'Hasn't him, and the like of him, got God's
voice in their hearts all day and they ever and always
listening to it. He'll wake of himself, you'll see. He'll
need no calling!'

And sure enough, as they were speaking, who came
running down the shingle but Seoineen.

'My father's not gone out without me, is he?' he
cried, not seeing their own boat, or any sign of it on the
shore, a cloud coming over his face that was all smiles
and laughter when he was running down to them. He
began to scan the bay that was blackened with boats by
this time.

'He's not then,' said Maurya. 'He's above in his bed
still, but leave him be, Seoineen — leave him be —' she
nodded her head back towards the shade of the promontory. 'He tarred the boat yesterday, not knowing the
seed 'ud be in so soon, and it would scald the heart out of
him to be here and not able to take it out. But as I was
saying to these good people it's maybe God's will the way
it's happened, because he's not fit to go out this day!'

'That's true for you, Mother,' said Seoineen, quietly.
'The poor man is nearly beat, I'm fearing.' But the next
minute he threw back his head and looked around the
shore. 'Maybe I'd get an oar in one of the other boats.
There's surely a scarcity of men these days?'

'Is it you?' cried his mother, because it mortally

offended her notion of the dignity due to him that he'd
be seen with his coat off maybe — in his shirt sleeves
maybe — red in the face maybe along with that and —
God forbid — sweat maybe breaking out of him!

'To hear you, Mother, anyone would think I was a
priest already. I wish you could get a look into the
seminary and you'd see there's a big difference made
there between the two sides of the fence!' It was clear
from the light in his eyes as they swept the sea at that
moment that it would take more than a suit of black clothes
to stop him from having a bit of fun with an oar. He gave a
sudden big laugh, but it fell away as sudden when he saw
that all the boats had pulled out from the shore and he
was alone with the women on the sand.

Then his face hardened.

'Tell me, Mother,' he cried. 'Is it the boat or my
father that's the unfittest? For if it's only the boat then I'll
make it fit! It would be going against God's plenitude
to stay idle with the sea teeming like that — Look at it!'

For even from where they stood when the waves
wheeled inward they could see the silver herring seed
glistening in the curving wheels of water, and when those
slow wheels broke on the shore they left behind them a
spate of seed sticking to everything, even to people's
shoes.

'And for that matter, wasn't Christ Himself a fisher-
man! Come, Mother — tell me the truth! Is the tar
still wet or is it not?'

Maurya looked at him for a minute. She was no
match for arguing with him in matters of theology, but
she knew all about tarring a currach. 'Wasn't it only
done yesterday, son,' she said. 'How could it be dry
today?'

'We'll soon know that,' said Seoineen, and he ran over
to the currach. Looking after him they saw him lay the
palm of his hand flat on the upturned bottom of the

boat, and then they heard him give a shout of exultation.

'It's not dry surely?' someone exclaimed, and you could tell by the faces that all were remembering the way he prophesied about the catch. Had the tar dried at the touch of his hands maybe?

But Seoineen was dragging the currach down the shingle.

'Why wouldn't it be dry?' he cried. 'Wasn't it a fine dry night. I remember going to the door after talking to my father into the small hours, and the sky was a mass of stars, and there was a fine, sharp wind blowing that you'd be in dread it would dry up the sea itself! Stand back there, Mother,' he cried, for her face was beseeching something of him, and he didn't want to be looking at it. But without looking he knew what it was trying to say. 'Isn't it towards my ordination the money is going? Isn't that argument enough for you?'

He had the boat nearly down to the water's edge. 'No, keep back there, young Jimeen,' he said. 'I'm able to manage it on my own, but let you get the nets and put them in and then be ready to skip in before I push out, because I'll need someone to help haul in the nets.'

'Is it Jimeen?' said one of the women, and she laughed, and then all the women laughed. 'Sure, he's more precious again nor you!' they said.

But they turned to his mother all the same.

'If you're ever going to let him go out at all, this is your one chance, surely? Isn't it like as if it was into the Hands of God Himself you were putting him, woman?'

'Will you let me, Ma?' It was the biggest moment in his life. He couldn't look at her for fear of a refusal.

'Come on, didn't you hear her saying yes — what are you waiting for?' cried Seoineen, giving him a push, and the next minute he was in the currach, and Seoineen had given it a great shove and he running out into the water

in his fine shoes and all. He vaulted in across the keel.
'I'm destroyed already at the very start!' he cried, laughing down at his feet and trouser legs, and that itself
seemed part of the sport for him. 'I'll take them off,' he
cried, kicking the shoes off him, and pulling off his socks,
till he was in his bare white feet. 'Give me the oars,' he
cried, but as he gripped them he laughed again, and loosed
his fingers for a minute, as one after the other, he rubbed
his hands on a bit of sacking on the seat beside him. For,
like the marks left by the trawler men on the white
bollard at the pier, the two bleached oars were marked
with the track of his hands, palms, and fingers, in pitch
black tar.

'The tar was wet!'

'And what of it?' cried Seoineen. 'Isn't it easy give
it another lick of a brush?'

But he wasn't looking at Jimeen and he saying it, his
eyes were lepping along the tops of the waves to see if they
were pulling near the other currachs.

The other currachs were far out in the bay already:
the sea was running strong. For all that, there was a
strange still look about the water, unbroken by any spray.
Jimeen sat still, exulting in his luck. The waves did not
slap against the sides of the currach like he'd have thought
they would do, and they didn't even break into spray
where the oars split their surface. Instead, they seemed
to go lolloping under the currach and lollop up again
the far side, till it might have been on great glass rollers
they were slipping along.

'God! Isn't it good to be out on the water!' cried
Seoineen, and he stood up in the currach, nearly toppling
them over in his exuberance, drawing in deep breaths,
first with his nose, and then as if he were drinking it with
his mouth, and his eyes at the same time taking big
draughts of the coast-line that was getting farther and
farther away. 'Ah, this is the life: this is the real life,' he

cried again, but they had to look to the oars and look to the nets, then, for a while, and for a while they couldn't look up at sea or sky.

When Jimeen looked up at last, the shore was only a narrow line of green.

'There's a bit of a change, I think,' said Seoineen, and it was true.

The waves were no longer round and soft, like the little cnoceens in the fields back of the shore, but they had small sharp points on them now, like the rocks around the Point, that would rip the bottom out of a boat with one tip, the way a tip of a knife would slit the belly of a fish.

That was a venomous comparison though and for all their appearance, when they hit against the flank of the boat, it was only the waves themselves that broke and patterned the water with splotches of spray.

It was while he was looking down at these white splotches that Jimeen saw the fish.

'Oh look, Seoineen, look!' he cried, because never had he seen the like.

They were not swimming free, or separate, like you'd think they'd be, but a great mass of them together, till you'd think it was at the floor of the sea you were looking, only it nearer and shallower.

There must have been a million fish; a million, million, Jimeen reckoned wildly, and they pressed as close as the pebbles on the shore. And they might well have been motionless and only seeming to move like on a windy day you'd think the grass on the top of the promontory was running free like the waves, with the way it rippled and ran along a little with each breeze.

'Holy God, such a sight!' cried Seoineen. 'Look at them!'

But Jimeen was puzzled.

'How will we get them into the net?' he asked, because it didn't seem that there was any place for the net to slip down between them, but that it must lie on the top of that solid mass of fish, like on a floor.

'The nets: begod, I nearly forgot what we came out here for!' cried Seoineen, and at the same time they became aware of the activity in the other boats, which had drawn near without their knowing. He yelled at Jimeen. 'Catch hold of the nets there, you lazy good-for-nothing. What did I bring you with me for if it wasn't to put you to some use!' and he himself caught at a length of the brown mesh, thrown in the bottom of the boat, and began to haul it up with one hand, and with the other to feed it out over the side.

Jimeen, too, began to pull and haul, so that for a few minutes there was only a sound of the net swishing over the wood, and every now and then a bit of a curse, under his breath, from Seoineen as one of the cork floats caught in the thole pins.

At first it shocked Jimeen to hear Seoineen curse, but he reflected that Seoineen wasn't ordained yet, and that, even if he were, it must be a hard thing for a man to go against his nature.

'Come on, get it over the side, damn you,' cried Seoineen again, as Jimeen had slowed up a bit owing to thinking about the cursing. 'It isn't one net-full but thirty could be filled this day! Sure you could fill the boat in fistfuls,' he cried, suddenly leaning down over the side, delving his bare hand into the water. With a shout, he brought up his hand with two fish, held one against the other in the same grip, so that they were as rigid as if they were dead. 'They're overlaying each other a foot deep,' he cried, and then he opened his fist and freed them. Immediately they writhed apart to either side of his hand in two bright arcs and then fell, both of them, into the bottom of the boat. But next moment they writhed into the air again, and flashed over the side of the currach.

'Ah begorras, you'll get less elbow-room there than

here, my boys,' cried Seoineen, and he roared laughing, as he and Jimeen leant over the side, and saw that sure enough, the two mackerel were floundering for a place in the glut of fishes.

But a shout in one of the other currachs made them look up.

It was the same story all over the bay. The currachs were tossing tipsily in the water with the antics of the crews, that were standing up and shouting and feeding the nets ravenously over the sides. In some of the boats that had got away early, they were still more ravenously hauling them up, strained and swollen with the biggest catch they had ever held.

There was not time for Seoineen or Jimeen to look around either, for just then the keel of their own currach began to dip into the water.

'Look out! Pull it up—! Catch a better grip than that, damn you. Do you want to be pulled into the sea. Pull, damn you, pull!' cried Seoineen.

Now every other word that broke from his throat was a curse, or what you'd call a curse if you heard them from another man, or in another place, but in this place, from this man, hearing them issue wild and free, Jimeen understood that they were a kind of psalm. They rang out over the sea in a kind of praise to God for all his plenitude.

'Up! Pull hard — up, now, up!' he cried, and he was pulling at his end like a madman.

Jimeen pulled too, till he thought his heart would crack, and then suddenly the big white belly of the loaded net came in sight over the water.

Jimeen gave a groan, though, when he saw it.

'Is it dead they are?' he cried, and there was anguish in his voice.

Up to this, the only live fish he had ever seen were the few fish tangled in the roomy nets, let down by the old men over the end of the pier, and *they* were always full of life, needling back and forth insanely in the spacious mesh till he used to swallow hard, and press his lips close together fearing one of them would dart down his gullet, and he'd have it ever after needling this way and that inside him! But there was no stir at all in the great white mass that had been hauled up now in the nets.

'Is it dead they are?' he cried again.

'Aahh, why would they be dead? It's suffocating they are, even below in the water, with the welter of them is in it,' cried Seoineen.

He dragged the net over the side where it emptied and spilled itself into the bottom of the boat. They came alive then all right! Flipping and floundering, and some of them flashing back into the sea. But it was only a few on the top that got away, the rest were kept down by the very weight and mass of them that was in it. And when, after a minute, Seoineen had freed the end of the net, he flailed them right and left till most of them fell back flat. Then, suddenly, he straightened up and swiped a hand across his face to clear it of the sweat that was pouring out of him.

'Ah sure, what harm if an odd one leps for it,' he cried. 'We'll deaden them under another netful! Throw out your end,' he cried.

As Jimeen rose up to his full height to throw the net wide out, there was a sudden terrible sound in the sky over him, and the next minute a bolt of thunder went volleying overhead, and with it, in the same instant it seemed, the sky was knifed from end to end with a lightning flash.

Were they blinded by the flash? Or had it suddenly gone as black as night over the whole sea?

'Oh God's Cross!' cried Seoineen. 'What is coming? Why didn't someone give us a shout? Where are the others? Can you see them? Hoy there! Marteen! Seumas? Can you hear—?'

For they could see nothing. And it was as if they were all alone in the whole world. Then, suddenly, they made out Marteen's currach near to them, so near that, but for Seoineen flinging himself forward and grabbing the oars, the two currachs would have knocked together. Yet no sooner had they been saved from knocking together than they suddenly seemed so far sundered again they could hardly hear each other when they called out.

'What's happening, in Christ's name?' bawled Seoineen, but he had to put up his hands to trumpet his voice, for the waves were now so steep and high that even one was enough to blot out the sight of Marteen. Angry white spume dashed in their faces.

'It's maybe the end of the world,' said Jimeen, terror-stricken.

'Shut up and let me hear Marteen!' said Seoineen, for Marteen was bawling at them again.

'Let go the nets,' Marteen was bawling — 'let go the nets or they'll drag you out of the boat.'

Under them then they could feel the big pull of the net that was filled up again in an instant with its dead weight of suffocating fish.

'Let it go, I tell you,' bawled Marteen.

'Did you hear? He's telling us to let it go,' piped Jimeen in terror, and he tried to free his own fingers of the brown mesh that had closed tight upon them with the increasing weight. 'I can't let go,' he cried, looking to Seoineen, but he shrank back from the strange wild look in Seoineen's eyes. 'Take care would you do anything of the kind!'

'It's cutting off my fingers!' he screamed.

Seoineen glared at him.

'A pity about them!' he cried, but when he darted a look at them, and saw them swelling and reddening, he cursed. 'Here — wait till I take it from you,' he cried, and he went to free his own right hand, but first he laced the laden fingers of his left hand into the mesh above the right hand, and even then, the blood spurted out in the air when he finally dragged it free of the mesh.

For a minute Seoineen shoved his bleeding fingers into his mouth and sucked them, then he reached out and caught the net below where Jimeen gripped it. As the weight slackened, the pain of the searing strings lessened, but next minute as the pull below got stronger, the pain tore into Jimeen's flesh again.

'Let go now, if you like, now I have a bit of a hold of it anyway — now I'm taking the weight of it off you,' said Seoineen.

Jimeen tried to drag free.

'I can't,' he screamed in terror, '— the strings are eating into my bones!'

Seoineen altered his balance and took more weight off the net at that place.

'Now!'

'I can't! I can't!' screamed Jimeen.

From far over the waves the voice of Marteen came to them again, faint, unreal, like the voices you'd hear in a shell if you held it to your ear.

'Cut free — cut free,' it cried, 'or else you'll be destroyed altogether.'

'Have they cut free themselves? That's what I'd like to know?' cried Seoineen.

'Oh, do as he says, Seoineen. Do as he says,' screamed Jimeen.

And then, as he saw a bit of ragged net, and then another and another rush past like the briery patches of foam on the water that was now almost level with the rowlocks, he knew that they had indeed all done what Marteen said; cut free.

'For the love of God, Seoineen,' he cried.

Seoineen hesitated for another instant. Then suddenly made up his mind and, reaching along the seat, he

felt without looking for the knife that was kept there for
slashing dogfish.

'Here goes,' he cried, and with one true cut of the
knife he freed Jimeen's hands the two together at the
same time, but, letting the knife drop into the water, he
reached out wildly to catch the ends of the net before they
slid into it, or shed any of their precious freight.

Not a single silver fish was lost.

'What a fool I'd be,' he gasped, 'to let go. They
think because of the collar I haven't a man's strength
about me any more. Then I'll show them. I'll not let
go this net, not if it pull me down to hell.' And he gave
another wild laugh. 'And you along with me!' he cried.
'Murder?' he asked then, as if he had picked up the
word from a voice in the wind. 'Is it murder? Ah sure,
I often think it's all one to God what a man's sin is, as
long as it's sin at all. Isn't sin poison — any sin at all,
even the smallest drop of it? Isn't it death to the soul that
it touches at any time? Ah then! I'll not let go!' And
even when, just then, the whole sea seemed littered with
tattered threads of net, he still held tight to his hold. 'Is
that the way? They've all let go! Well then, I'll show
them one man will not be so easy beat! Can you hear
me?' he cried, because it was hard to hear him with the
crazy noise of the wind and the waves.

'Oh cut free, Seoineen,' Jimeen implored, although
he remembered the knife was gone now to the bottom of
the sea, and although the terrible swollen fingers were
beyond help in the mangling ropes of the net.

'Cut free is it? Faith now! I'll show them all,' cried
Seoineen. 'We'll be the only boat'll bring back a catch this
night, and the sea seething with fish. He gave a laugh.
'Sure that was the only thing that was spoiling my pleasure
in the plenty! thinking that when the boats got back the
whole island would be fuller of fish than the sea itself, and it
all of no more value than if it was washed of its own accord

on to the dirty counters of the shop! Sure it wouldn't be worth a farthing a barrel! But it will be a different story now, I'm thinking. Oh, but I'll have the laugh on them with their hollow boats, and their nets cut to flitters! I'll show them a man is a man, no matter what vows he takes, or what way he's called to deny his manhood! I'll show them! Where are they, anyway? Can you — see them — at all?' he cried, but he had begun to gasp worse than the fishes in the bottom of the boat. 'Can you — see them — at all? Damn you, don't sit there like that! Stand up — there — and tell me — can — you — see — them!'

It wasn't the others Jimeen saw though, when he raised his eyes from the torn hands in the meshes. All he saw was a great wall, a great green wall of water. No currachs anywhere. It was as if the whole sea had been stood up on its edge, like a plate on a dresser. And down that wall of water there slid a multitude of dead fish.

And then, down the same terrible wall, sliding like the dead fish, came an oar; a solitary oar. And a moment afterwards, but inside the glass wall, imprisoned, like under a glass dome, he saw — oh God! — a face, looking out at him, staring out at him through a foot of clear green water. And he saw it was the face of Marteen. For a minute the eyes of the dead man stared into his eyes.

With a scream he threw himself against Seoineen, and clung to him tight as iron.

How many years ago was that? The Bishop opened his eyes. They were so near the shore he could pick out the people by name that stood on the pier-head. His stomach had stopped rolling. It was mostly psychological; that feeling of nausea. But he knew it would come back in an instant if he looked leftward from the shore, leftwards and upwards, where, over the little cement pier and over the crane-bill steeple of the church, the promontory that they called the Point rose up black with its own shadow.

For it was on that promontory — four times the height of the steeple — they had found themselves, he and Seoineen, in the white dawn of the day after the Wave, lying in a litter of dead fish, with the netful of fish like an anchor sunk into the green grass.

When he came to himself in that terrible dawn, and felt the slippy bellies of the fish all about him, he thought he was still in the boat, lying in the bottom among the mackerel, but when he opened his eyes and saw a darkness as of night, over his head, he thought it was still the darkness of the storm and he closed them again in terror.

Just before he closed them, though, he thought he saw a star, and he ventured to open them again, and then he saw that the dark sky over him was a sky of skin, stretched taut over timber laths, and the star was only a glint of light — and the blue light of day at that — coming through a split in the bottom of the currach. For the currach was on top of him ! — Not he in the bottom of it.

Why then was he not falling down and down and down through the green waters ? His hands rushed out to feel around him. But even then, the most miraculous thing he thought to grasp was a fistful of sand, the most miracu- lous thing he thought to have to believe was that they were cast up safe upon the shore.

Under his hands though, that groped through the fishes, he came, not on sand, but on grass, and not upon the coarse dune grass that grew back from the shore at the foot of the Point. It was soft, sweet little grass, that was like the grass he saw once when Seoineen and he had climbed up the face of the Point, and stood up there, in the sun, looking down at all below, the sea and the pier, and the shore and the fields, and the thatch of their own houses, and on a level with them, the grey spire of the chapel itself !

It was, when opening his eyes wide at last, he saw, out

from him a bit, the black grey tip of that same chapel-spire that he knew where he was.

Throwing the fish to left and right he struggled to get to his feet.

It was a miracle! And it must have been granted because Seoineen was in the boat. He remembered how he prophesied the seed would be on the tide, and in his mind he pictured their currach being lifted up in the air and flown, like a bird, to this grassy point.

But where was Seoineen?

'Oh Seoineen, Seoineen!' he cried, when he saw him standing on the edge of the Point looking downward, like they looked, that day, on all below. 'Oh Seoineen, was it a miracle?' he cried, and he didn't wait for an answer, but he began to shout and jump in the air.

'Quit, will you!' said Seoineen, and for a minute he thought it must be modesty on Seoineen's part, it being through him the miracle was granted, and then he thought it must be the pain in his hands that was at him, not letting him enjoy the miracle, because he had his two hands pressed under his armpits.

Then suddenly he remembered the face of Marteen he had seen under the wall of water, and his eyes flew out over the sea that was as flat and even now, as the field of grass under their feet. Was Marteen's currach lost? And what of the others?

Craning over the edge of the promontory he tried to see what currachs were back in their places, under the little wall, dividing the sand from the dune, turned upside down and leaning a little to one side, so you could crawl under them if you were caught in a sudden shower.

There were no currachs under the wall: none at all.

There were no currachs on the sea.

Once, when he was still wearing a red petticoat like a girsha, there had been a terrible storm and half a score of currachs were lost. He remembered the night with all

the women on the island down on the shore with storm
lamps, swinging them and calling out over the noise of the
waves. And the next day they were still there, only kneeling on the pier, praying and keening.

'Why aren't they praying and keening?' he cried
then, for he knew at last the other currachs, all but their's,
were lost.

'God help them,' said Seoineen, 'at least they were
spared that.'

And he pointed to where, stuck in the latticed shutters
on the side of the steeple, there were bits of seaweed,
and — yes — a bit of the brown mesh of a net.

'God help you,' he said then, 'how can your child's
mind take in what a grown man's mind can hardly hold
— but you'll have to know some time — we're all alone —
the two of us — on the whole island. All that was spared
by that wall of water——'

'All that was on the sea, you mean?' he cried.

'And on the land too,' said Seoineen.

'Not my mother——?' he whimpered.

'Yes, and my poor mother,' said Seoineen. 'My poor
mother that tried to stop us from going out with the rest.'

But it was a grief too great to grasp, and yet, yet
even in face of it, Jimeen's mind was enslaved to the
thought of their miraculous salvation.

'Was it a miracle, Seoineen?' he whispered. 'Was it
a miracle we were spared?'

But Seoineen closed his eyes, and pushed his crossed
arms deeper under his arm-pits. The grimace of pain he
made was — even without words — a rebuke to Jimeen's
exaltation. Then he opened his eyes again.

'It was my greed that was the cause of all,' he said,
and there was such a terrible sorrow in his face that
Jimeen, only then, began to cry. 'It has cost me my two
living hands,' said Seoineen, and there was a terrible
anguish in his voice.

'But it saved your life, Seoineen,' he cried, wanting to comfort him.

Never did he forget the face Seoineen turned to him.

'For what?' he asked. 'For what?'

And there was, in his voice, such despair, that Jimeen knew it wasn't a question but an answer; so he said no more for a few minutes. Then he raised his voice again, timidly.

'You saved my life too, Seoineen.'

Seoineen turned dully and looked at him.

'For what?'

But as he uttered them, those same words took on a change, and a change came over his face, too, and when he repeated them, the change was violent.

'For what?' he demanded. 'For what?'

Just then, on the flat sea below, Jimeen saw the boats, coming across from the mainland, not currachs like they had on the island, but boats of wood made inland, in Athlone, and brought down on lorries.

'Look at the boats,' he called out, four, five, six, any amount of them; they came rowing for the island.

Less than an hour later Seoineen was on his way to the hospital on the mainland, where he was to spend long months before he saw the island again. Jimeen was taken across a few hours later, but when he went it was to be for good. He was going to an aunt, far in from the sea, of whom he had never heard tell till that day.

Nor was he to see Seoineen again, in all the years that followed. On the three occasions that he was over on the island, he had not seen him. He had made enquiries, but all he could ever get out of people was that he was a bit odd.

'And why wouldn't he be?' they added.

But although he never came down to the pier to greet the Bishop like the rest of the islanders, it was said he used to slip into the church after it had filled up and he'd think he was unnoticed. And afterwards, although he never once would go down to the pier to see the boat off, he never went back into his little house until it was gone clear across to the other side of the bay. From some part of the island it was certain he'd be the last to take leave of the sight.

It had been the same on each visit the Bishop made, and it would be the same on this one.

When he would be leaving the island, there would be the same solicitous entreaties with him to put on his overcoat. Certainly he was always colder going back in the late day. But he'd never give in to do more than throw it over his shoulders, from which it would soon slip down on to the seat behind him.

'You'd do right to put it on like they told you,' said the secretary, buttoning up his own thick coat.

But there was no use trying to make him do a thing he was set against. He was a man had deep reasons for the least of his actions.

The Mouse

LEILA wasn't my real aunt at all, although I called her Aunt Leila in affection. She was only a dear friend of my mother. They were girls together, not, I gather, such *very* great friends at all, but when my father died and my mother came back to her home town, the friendship really developed. Aunt Leila being an old maid, you see, and Mother being a widow, they were in greater need of each other's company than when they were young, and separated by their hopes and dreams.

They saw a certain amount of each other, of course, even in those days, because they were the only three girls in their town who went by train each day to the convent school in Galway. They had a pass on the railway, the three of them: my mother, and Leila, and Mina.

Mina was never a friend of my mother. Indeed, they disliked each other. My mother said so straight out one day to Leila.

'I *never* liked her, Leila as you know. I never could understand what you saw in her.'

And Leila sighed.

'It just was to be, I suppose,' she said, and her face was so sad that later, when she had gone, I asked my mother about it.

She hesitated for a minute.

'Well, there's no reason why you shouldn't know — what little there is to know. You see, Leila was going to be married one time, to a most suitable person too, and then — well — no one knew exactly what happened, but one night he eloped with Mina. Leila behaved wonderfully. Nobody ever heard her say a word against either

26

of them. Not a word. Can you imagine that!' cried my
mother. 'Wouldn't you think she'd just have to unbur-
then herself to someone? We may not have been bosom
friends in those days, but she could have told *me*. Yet
their names never passed her lips. It was very strange.
The whole town was a hive of gossip. Everyone wanted
to know what had happened, but all they could make out
was that there was a bit of an estrangement between
Arthur and Leila, and that he was seen talking to Mina
a few times, but no more than that! Nothing to explain
the next thing that happened, the two of them eloping —
Mina and Arthur, I mean —— and getting married in
Dublin. Poor Leila: even now it seems hard to believe
it happened.'

'But why didn't she marry someone else?' I cried.
'She must have been very good-looking.'

'She was!' cried my mother. 'She was absolutely
lovely; a most striking face, as you can still see, but unfortunately as she said to me recently, *she didn't know it.*'

I didn't see how that counted for anything.

'Oh, it made all the difference in the world,' cried my
mother. 'Why, even that awful Mina, who was hardly
to be called pretty, even in the commonest way, was so
well read about her own looks that I used to think she'd
know how to show herself off to the best advantage if she
were to be laid out dead! Oh that one! She was good-
looking, I'll admit: but there was a lot of trickery to
that one's looks. Whereas Leila had a kind of unregarding
beauty that was there *all* the time, no matter whether it
was being shown up or not. If she took any thought of it,
she could have dazzled people. Not that I think she
would have liked dazzling anyone. I think that, no
matter what happened, it might have been a matter of
luck for the right person to come along. She was a kind
of person that you would have to put something into,
before there'd be anything to get back from her, if that's

not beyond you to understand? That was what Arthur did, you see.

'We all noticed the change in her when he began to walk out with her. We all saw suddenly that she had a beautiful face, and we hadn't realized it. But it wasn't everyone would have acted on her like Arthur, and that's why it was so terrible when that awful Mina got mixed up with them. Only for her, they'd be happily married today, like me — like I was, I mean.'

'All the same, it's a wonder she didn't marry someone else,' I said quickly, 'if she was so good-looking.'

'You poor child,' said my mother, 'you don't understand. She couldn't possibly have married anyone else. They were made for each other, she and Arthur: made for each other! It was like your father and me! You might as well think I'd have married someone else if *he* had jilted *me*.'

I'm afraid I took this avowal lightly. I wouldn't say there was a lot to choose between Mother and Mina when it came to having boys, just that Mother was a nice girl, and Mina — well, of course, I didn't know her, but she didn't *seem* nice, that's all. Whereas Leila — ah, there was someone who might easily be the kind of person to give her heart once, and once only.

'You see, Arthur was a bit of a stick really,' my mother went on. 'At least, that's how he appeared to us at first. I don't think I told you that I used to know *him* too, long ago, when we were going in and out to school on the train every day. There were three of us girls — I told you that — but there were five boys as well, although they travelled in a separate compartment. They were always pulling our plaits and jeering at us, and showing off before us too, but they never mixed with us all the same. They wouldn't be caught dead in the same compartment as us. I remember once one of them was late — I do believe it was Arthur! — and he came running on to the platform

as the guard was locking the doors, and what did the guard
do but open the door of our carriage and shove him in on
top of us. Oh, such laughing : we nearly died laughing,
but when Arthur saw it was our compartment, he wrenched
open the door again and jumped down on the line, although the train was moving fairly fast. He nearly broke
his neck. And the Stationmaster half killed him, and,
needless to say, he missed school that day on top of everything else : but he'd suffer all that rather than have the
indignity of travelling with us girls. He was always sort
of shy. Not but that the others would have acted the
same, and some of them were a long way from knowing
the meaning of shyness. There was one big fellow — I
forget his name, but if you knew what Mina told me —
but here mother stopped, '— looking back on it,' she said,
'I suppose Mina could have made up that story, or the
half of it anyway. But I know there was something gentler
about Arthur than there was about the others, although
to tell you the truth, I don't remember much about him,
and he was only a short time going in and out on the train.
He wasn't living in the town, you see, only staying with
people who lived in a big house on the outskirts. His own
people were abroad, or something — I don't remember —
but in any case he went back wherever he belonged after
a bit — I forget where — somewhere in Enniskillen, I
think — not that it matters. And he went clean out of
my thoughts, and out of Leila's too, I'm sure, because it
was only a coincidence that he came back to the town
later. There must be dozens of branches of the Ulster
Bank in the Twenty-six Counties ! But there you are ! It
was to our town he was sent. Can you blame us for
thinking it was Fate ? And when we heard Leila's mother
was going to take him as a paying guest, well, anyone
could guess what would happen !
'To begin with, they were both Protestants, did I tell
you that ? And then they were both the moody type —

quiet, and willing to say nothing if they weren't pressed. They were great readers, too — both of them. I like a good book myself, but if I take one up I can't put it down — it's the story I'm after, you see — but I often saw Leila take up a book — any book! — and start reading it — anywhere — in the middle or the end — anywhere, just for the sake of reading! And he was the same. And such books as he had in his room — Leila took me in one day — not a novel among them — would you believe it? And he was finished his studies at that time. It wasn't compulsory I mean, if that's what you're thinking. Not that Leila thought it remarkable. It wasn't to show me the books she took me into the room, but for some other reason, which I forget as a matter of fact, but looking back now I think it might only have been for the pleasure of going into his room. Would you believe it? I think she'd be too shy to go into it alone, and he away on his holidays in Enniskillen! That was Leila!

'It wouldn't be Mina's way, I can tell you. And talking about books, do you know I only saw that one with a book in her hands on one occasion, and it turned out to be one that, when you opened the cover, wasn't a book at all but a cigarette box! You couldn't imagine two people more unlike than Mina and him. But Leila and he looked sort of alike. I noticed it right away, a few days after he came to the town, when I saw them in the street. Don't laugh. Why shouldn't people be a bit alike outside if they can be exactly alike inside like those two?

'Arthur was good-looking, too, you see, in an odd way. I would even go so far as to say that, like Leila, he was the kind, too, who was better looking than you'd think at first sight. I know if he had half the notions about himself that some men had, he'd have put more oil in his hair, for one thing, and not have it sticking up like a sweeping brush. Most people saw the shock of yellow hair on him before they saw what good features he had.

'I remember Mina laughing the first time *she* saw him.

'That was the funny part of it. Mina didn't think anything of him at first. We were all dying to see what the new bank clerk would be like, and of course Mina — trust her! — was the first to clap eyes on him. 'Towpate : that's his name, girls,' she said, when she came back from some trumped-up message at the bank. She didn't even recognize him, or know she'd ever seen him before in her life. And when she heard Leila's mother wás having him in the house as a paying guest, she pitied Leila.

' "Isn't it a shame," she said to me, "that when Leila's mother got it into her head to take a lodger, that she didn't get somebody eligible. Because you know, Leila will never marry anyone — she'll be an old maid for certain — unless somebody is thrown at her head — there'd be some hope for her in propinquity !"

'Oh, she was very well up, Mina. But it wasn't propinquity that brought Arthur and Leila together, of course — because I suppose that implies only a sexual attraction, and really, I sometimes thought that was one thing they didn't have at all ! It would have come, of course. Oh, it would have come for certain when they were married, which would have made everything perfect, but I don't think it was there at the time, unfortunately for Leila—'

And here my mother stopped.

'I wonder if I ought to be talking to you like this at all,' she said, dubiously, 'but then, you young people nowadays seem to know all that's to be known about everything without ever being told !' She sighed. 'Anyway, that's all that's to the story, so there's no harm done.'

'You mean you don't know what happened ?'

I never felt more let down in my life.

'I told you she never mentioned his name,' said my mother, with asperity.

'But perhaps Mina——?'

'As if I'd demean myself by talking about it to *her*,' said Mother. 'And anyway, who'd believe *her* version?'

'Do you know something, Mother?' I cried suddenly. 'You ought to ask Leila what happened — ask her *now*!'

'Are you out of your mind?' said my mother. 'When I kept my mouth shut at the time, I'm hardly likely to bring it up now, when she's mostly forgotten it, I hope.'

'She's not forgotten it,' I said. 'You'd know by a certain look in her face. Oh mother, it was wonderful of you not to have said anything to her then — at the time, I mean — but somehow I think it's almost unkind never to refer to it *now*. You see *now*, it's all she has ever had, or ever will have; that romance, and even if it never came to anything in the eyes of other people, it must comfort her to feel her life wasn't always empty and cold! Oh, I *do* think you ought to bring it up some day. It would be like talking about the dead — you said it yourself about Father! — they are only really dead when they are no longer remembered by the living — and it may be the same with Leila. You might be able to put a little more reality into her memories.'

'I never thought of that,' said my mother. 'And after all, there was a good deal of reality in it. Arthur *did* love her, I know that for certain. And he never loved Mina — I told you that, didn't I? — the marriage was an awful failure — I haven't heard anything about them for a long time. They left the town after a few years. I knew from the start it could never be the way it should be. So maybe, in a way, Leila ought to be made to feel she had more than Mina in the long run. Oh, the past is a queer place surely! I think sometimes, it's like what we're told to believe Heaven is like, with no marriage, and no giving in marriage, I mean the bodily memories die away, and you only remember the love after a while. If it weren't for that, the pain of love would be unbearable. Perhaps I hadn't so much more than Leila myself when all is said and done. It was only Mina who had less; less than either of us. You're right about talking to her : I will.'

And I knew she would. So that evening, when I was out for a cycle-run, and passed Mother and Leila pacing slowly along the country road, I didn't get off the bicycle, but just waved as if I was going somewhere, because I knew they were deep in it. Indeed, mother gave me one of her flashing blue glances that conveyed all and more than she wished to convey.

It was a beautiful evening. I cycled for miles, but I wasn't really going anywhere in particular, and there was only the one road back, so I had to pass them again whether I liked it or not. They were still walking up and down when I passed the second time. I was a bit embarrassed, but I don't think Leila noticed me at all. Mother saw me all right ; but the look she gave me wasn't at all the same as earlier in the evening. Even flying past on the bicycle, I could see she was impatient, not only with Leila, but with me. The evening was coming down, and it was chilly for all that it was spring. She was probably cold, I thought, walking up and down the road, and so slowly too.

When she did come home, about an hour later, her hands were icy. And she was inclined to be irritable with me.

'I hope you're satisfied,' she said. 'I'm two hours listening to her. And what about? I'll tell you! About nothing! All about nothing!' she cried, as she threw off her coat and began to fill the kettle for a cup of tea.

'Look —!' Suddenly she put down the kettle, and left the tap running gaily. 'Look! You wouldn't think

Leila was a bit — a bit strange, dear, would you? — from thinking about the past too much?'

'Hadn't you better tell me what happened first?'

'But that's what I'm trying to tell you: nothing happened; only she thinks the nothing was something! Oh dear, it was so hard to follow her, and she went on and on, once she started, and my shoe was hurting, and it was getting cold, and I don't see that it did any good, one way or another. Not that I'm sorry I spoke to her, because you were right, you know, about how precious the memories were to her, and I could see that my remembering them too made a difference to her. She said so. She said she sometimes found herself doubting that there had ever been anything between them. She began to wonder if she had only invented the things he said, just to fill up the terrible vacancy in her heart. Like as if she was getting queer, she meant, I suppose. I was so glad to be able to reassure her. Because, of course, everyone knew how he loved her. "It was plain to be seen in his eyes when he looked at you, Leila," I said. "And he was so manly about it, walking along the roads with you, right from the start, where another fellow would be afraid of getting named along with you." The tears came into her eyes when I said that.'

' "Oh, those evenings," she cried, and she lifted her head — you know how lovely she can look even now? — and it was like as if the same sweetness was in the air for her still. "Oh, those evenings," she cried. "We were only getting to know each other then; only talking about books." And she laughed.

' "Just the same!" I said. "It was manly of him, to be so open about you; and later in the summer, when you *really* were caught up with each other, it impressed everyone the way you still walked out together in the daylight, and sat down on the banks by the side of the road for everyone to see you together, although you

weren't engaged really, were you? I mean, you hadn't a
ring from him. There was something so innocent about
you both."

' "Too innocent maybe," she said quietly, and then
she started to talk in earnest.

' "Mina passed that remark, you know," she said,
quickly. "Only Mina had an ugly way of saying things,
and yet, do you know, I often wondered afterwards if she
was trying to warn me: warn me against herself even!
There was one day she met us on the road.

' "Well, you two don't deserve to live in a place like
this," she said, "with all the little lovers' lanes and shady
paths there are! I know where *I*'d go if I was spooning."
I remember she looked queerly at us: at me in particular.
I think it was that day she first got interested in Arthur.
After that we met her once or twice in about the same
place, and she was always alone, and that wasn't like
Mina. She'd stop when she came to where we'd be
sitting, and she'd sit down on the bank on the other side
of Arthur, and sometimes she stayed with us till it was
nearly time to go home.

' "I mustn't spoil sport," she'd say then. I always
thought that was a vulgar expression — a bit common —
but I think there was more than commonness in it when
Mina said it. I think she was sneering at me. But maybe
I was wronging her.

' "Another day she said it was well for us to be so
innocent. 'Have you nothing to hide at all?' she said.

' "We hadn't. And even now, even the way things
turned out, I'm still glad we were like that, and that
Arthur felt like that about me, wanting it to be all in the
sunlight, and out in the open. Yes! I'm glad, or I would
be only for one thing. Only one thing. I used to think
that if we were the kind that wanted to go down the lanes,
and climb through the hedges to the quiet of the fields,
Mina wouldn't have come on us, and hung around the

way she did! I suppose if I got time I'd have shaken her
off, but I got no time. It all happened so quickly. She
only joined us a few times at first, and even when she did
it two or three times running, it was all still less than a
week — a Thursday first, and then the Friday, and then
Saturday. It was the Saturday I felt really hurt, because
we were out for the whole afternoon. I thought she'd
see that that was different from our little walks in the
evenings, when we went out as much for the air as for anything else.

‘ "And as a matter of fact we weren't sitting on the
side of the road that day either. Do you know the first
field outside the ramparts, with the little stream running
through it? There are stones from the rampart fallen
into the water, and when it's sunny, the water sparkles
and sings going over them. It still does. But it was
heavenly that afternoon. The wall was all down in a
couple of places, and what did we do but climb over it
and sit down by the stream. I may have had it in the
back of my mind that Mina wouldn't see us if she passed.
Not that we weren't plain to be seen from the road, but
I thought she wouldn't think of looking across the wall.

‘ "But we weren't settled when I heard her voice."

‘ "Can I come in?" she cried, as if it was into a
parlour. And the next minute she flounced down beside
us.

‘ "I hope the ground isn't damp," she said. "My
mother told me not to sit down without something under
me. Give me that book, and I'll put it under me."

‘ "Arthur laughed."

‘ "Oh no, you won't," he said, snatching it away. He
had a great respect for books. "Anyway, the grass is
dry. Look at us sitting on it. I must say I didn't think
though that you were the kind of girl that would heed
all her mother's warnings."

‘ "Oh, not all of them!" said Mina, and she laughed.

And Arthur laughed again. "Anyway," said Mina, "she died when I was ten, so she didn't have time to warn me about everything."

'"Arthur laughed again. I never heard him laughing just like he did that day. But I was glad. Although it was his seriousness that I liked, I'd have loved to see him laughing too, if he felt like it. Even then, sitting there with Mina and me, he soon got serious again.

' "My mother died too when I was about ten."

' "Then you're in the same boat as me!" said Mina.

' "But I don't think he heard her."

' "I only remember one thing about my mother," he said. "When she came to say good-night to me, I used to hold up my face to be kissed, and then I used to hold out my wrist to her. 'Do the mouse! Do the mouse!' I'd say, because sometimes — not always — she used to put her hand up my sleeve and run her fingers over the inner side of my wrist where the veins are — pretending her fingers were little mice-feet."

' "Suddenly he pulled back the sleeve of his coat, and tugged at his cuff to show us his wrist.

' "I never forgot it," he said. "I don't know what age I was, but I hardly remember anything else about my mother; even what she looked like."

' "That was all he said about her, and we talked about other things. It was such a warm, soft day. Arthur lay back in the grass, looking up at the sky, and we two sat to either side of him. I think I did most of the talking. But Mina was quieter than usual, I remember that well.

' "I remember almost everything about that day like as if it was a painting, and I was outside it, instead of in it. I remember a man with an ass and cart came down to the bank of the stream where we were sitting, with a big barrel to fill for the cattle grazing inside the ramparts. Well, I suppose anyone would remember a thing like that, but I remember every detail of it, and how when the barrel was filled, and he was leading the ass up from the stream, the wheels of the cart rocked, and little silver drops of water were tossed up into the air, and they seemed to hang in the air for a minute, like a spray of tremble-grass, before they fell back into the barrel. Fancy remembering that all those years! And I remember, just close to Arthur's face once, where he was lying back in the grass, a little black insect — at least it must have been black, but it glinted green and gold and every colour in the sun — a little insect you'd hardly see, it was so small, started to climb up a blade of grass, a thin green blade, and then, just when it was near the tip, the blade bent in the middle and down it splashed into the meadow again.

' "Oh dear," I exclaimed, and the others looked at me.

' "It was only an insect," I said.

' "Arthur shook his head. 'I hope he doesn't crawl into my ear,' he said, but he wasn't greatly worried, and he threw back his arms over his head, palm-side upwards.

' "Perhaps it was the way they were palm upwards that put it into Mina's head to do what she did. Perhaps it was me talking about the insect that made Arthur start and sit up. But anyway, all of a sudden he sat up, and began to rub his wrist.

' "Something stung me," he said crossly.

' "Mina laughed.

' "It was only me," she said, and she leant over him. "I only did this," she said, and she dabbled her fingers in the air over his wrist: not even touching him at all this time. "I was doing the mouse," she said.

' "And that was a Saturday. We all walked home soon afterwards, and the following Monday they ran away, Arthur and Mina. And I never mentioned their names again to anyone: till now. I never told anyone about the mouse, because I don't see what it had to do with their running away, do you? And yet, it must have had something to do with it." '

My mother stopped talking suddenly and looked at me.

'Did you ever hear such a rigmarole?' she said. 'Could her mind be affected; that's what I want to know! Or can *you* make anything out of a story like that?'

Second-hand

IT was when it came to selling the clothes that Essy gave trouble, but Mae was able for her.

It wasn't only being older than her and being married; Mae was *always* the one with a bit of sense, and more than a bit indeed. Look at how well she had done for herself over in England. You could guess by the way she sat on the edges of the chairs in Clanbrassil Street that she was used to something a cut above this, anyway.

'There's no use talking, Essy,' she said. 'You've got to take some steps.'

There was never much money at any time, as Mae well knew. It was the same before she went away too — but there was none at all now — except the few pounds they found under poor Mother's own mattress. The pension died with the old woman.

'I don't know what you'd have done without this, Essy,' she said, as she gathered up the few dirty notes. 'You were sailing very near the wind, even with poor Mother alive, and the pension coming in to you!'

Such a position was unthinkable to Mae. As well it might be because, if it weren't for security, what had she got out of her marriage to Tom? All the use she could see in him now was that he kept the wolf from the door. But that was something after all. For without some money what would become of one? It was a question Essy never seemed to pose. She turned back in exasperation to her.

'You'll have to take lodgers, Essy. There's no way out of it! And before you go looking for them you'll have to get this place cleaned up a bit, and painted. *And* to do that you'll have to get hold of a few pounds more

from somewhere. So, for the first and last time, are you,
or are you not, going to let me sell those old clothes?'

They were standing in the back hall, that was darkened
and narrowed by an ungainly plush curtain of hairy
brown colour. Weighed with decades of dust, it may
have been the cause of a faint but pervasive odour of
decay so peculiar to the house.

'Open the back door there, Essy,' said Mae, sharply.
If there was light Essy might be made to see the nonsense
of treasuring up such rubbish. For behind the curtain
was a hallstand, on which hung a bulk of old clothes that
must have been accumulating for forty years!

'What would we get for them, I wonder?' mused Mae.
'What would we need to do up even one room? It would
take thirty shillings a day I'm sure at the very least, and
there must be three or four days' work in it. We'd have
to get a good price for the clothes, I can tell you, Essy!
I hope they are not musty or moth-eaten.' And she ap-
plied herself vigorously to the rack of clothes.

'My God, but there is a mountain of things here!
They can't all be yours and Mother's. Well! don't tell
me there are old things of mine here. Now *don't* tell me
that is my old blue coat! It is, I declare! Or is it yours?
Didn't you have one like it, Essy?'

'Mine is there too somewhere,' said Essy apathetically.
'Mother never minded what she threw across her back if
she was running out for a message at night.'

But Mae was rummaging among the old clothes as if
she were at a clearance sale.

'Oh no! This couldn't be the remains of that fur-
fabric coat I got with my first earnings, could it? Oh
dear! the hopes I had then.'

Suddenly she stopped rummaging.

'Can't you see, Essy, that selling these things has
nothing to do with Mother really? They're mostly our
own.'

'Mother bought them for us,' said Essy, doggedly. 'And it's so soon to start making changes.'

'It's soon all right.' Mae was prepared to cede that point. But she had to go back. She had only been spared for the funeral. Otherwise she would have enjoyed looking leisurely through the old things. 'I'll tell you what we'll do,' she said in an impulse of generosity. 'We'll get the paper-hanger started in the morning, and we'll see how far Mother's own money will stretch. How's that? Then we can decide about the clothes. How about that?' she repeated, gently, because of course she couldn't let herself forget that she owed something to Essy. The two of them couldn't have left Mother. And if Essy had been more alive to her position long ago — it might have been her who had the wit to flit, and she, Mae, the one to be left behind in Clanbrassil Street! 'How's that for a suggestion?' she repeated, still more kindly. 'Come and we'll make a pot of tea, and go down and get a paper-hanger this very evening.'

The tea was hot, and it made them both feel better. Essy too felt a wish to concede a little in sisterly affection.

'I suppose we could sort through the clothes anyway,' she said, 'whether we decided to sell them or not. We might even sell some of them, but not Mother's own things!'

As if those weren't the ones that were crying out to be sold, thought Mae, but she knew it was as well to humour Essy.

'We'll see,' she said. 'Who does the paper-hanging for you now?'

As she said it, she realized that the old wallpaper, which seemed to be brown roses on an orange background, but which must surely once have been pink on white, had been on the walls as long as she could remember, but Essy took the question to cover all Clanbrassil Street.

'Charlie Mack does it now,' she said.

'Well, come on down to his house,' said Mae. 'We'll fix up with him to come up as soon as he can — I suppose he's busy, but he might see this is an emergency.'

Charlie didn't seem to be all that busy, or putting it otherwise, as he did himself, he wasn't a slave to the clock, like the trade unionists. Even if he was busy he could put on a spurt.

'Hard work never killed anyone,' said Charlie. 'I wouldn't think twice of working all night if a job had to be done: but of course, your trade unionist won't do that; he can't do it: he'd be called to heel. When do you want me to come?'

'Would tomorrow morning——?'

'Righty-ho,' said Charlie. 'I'm in the middle of a big job, but I can switch it: the walls were a bit fresh for taking the paste anyway, or so I'll tell them!'

'I didn't know there were any workmen to be had outside the union,' said Essy. 'Mother never trusted the trade unions.'

Mae nodded in recognition of a remembered fact. But she looked sceptical all the same.

'It may be different here from England,' she said, 'but the unions aren't like what they were when Mother was young. Only the trouble-makers were in the unions then, but now I'd be more inclined to think it queer for a fellow to be outside them. He looked all right though, didn't he?'

And he could work! There was no doubt of that.

Bright and early next morning Charlie was rapping on the door, with his bucket and his ladder, and in a few seconds, his coat was off, and he was sloshing water over the walls. The room was stripped by dinner-time, and at half-past four he was looking for the kitchen table, to spread out the new paper on it. (Stripes this time, Mae insisted; it wouldn't matter what way the stripes faded.)

'Oh, he's a great worker,' she cried. 'It'll be done

before I go back, and maybe you'll have the lodger got as well, because I'm going to put an advertisement in the evening paper. Once the work is started, that's all that matters. But Essy, I have an idea. You'll have to let me sell those old clothes, because I was just thinking it's a shame to let this young fellow go without having him do the hall and maybe give a lick of paint to the hall-door, and the outside of the windows — he might even be able to give a dab to the railings. Think how it'd brighten up the place. I was thinking how shabby the outside of the house was the day of the funeral.'

'Oh no,' cried Essy. 'I hope it didn't spoil the effect of the funeral, because I was thinking how Mother would have been proud of everything that day.' And then, with her balmy, far-away look that Mae knew so well, Essy smiled. 'I'd be the same,' she said. Then she came back to earth. 'How much would we get for the clothes, do you think?' she said crisply and in a business-like way.

'To sort them is the first step to finding that out,' said Mae, quickly. 'Come on,' she cried. 'Oh see, the hall-curtain is down. There'll be more light.'

For Charlie had stripped the hall, while he was waiting for the walls in the parlour to dry. Indeed, he had taken down all the things from the hall-rack and heaped them on the floor : a heap as high as a haystack.

'They don't look so personal, somehow, do they?' said Mae.

Indeed, as she lifted up one or two of the things from the top, which had been buried at the bottom of the pile when they still hung on the hooks, she hardly recognized them as anything belonging to them. She almost had a distaste for handling them, and when she lifted the top garment she picked it up delicately, and held it out from her with the tips of her fingers.

Disturbed, brought out into the living air, there

seemed to be a smell from the old clothes, like the smell that comes out from a second-hand clothes shop. She felt like holding her nose.

'Let's bundle them up quick — will we?' she cried. 'We won't sort them at all. Is there anything that's your own? I mean anything that you really could still wear — here, what about this?' she cried, as something a bit less shabby — and less smelly if you like — came to light. 'A gaberdine coat, is it?'

'It's not mine,' said Essy. 'I didn't have gaberdine since I was at school,' and she didn't bother to look up. 'There was an old oilskin here though, that might be useful on a really wet day.'

'Now, don't enter into temptation, Essy,' cried Mae, gaily. She was still looking at the gaberdine. 'It's almost new,' she said. It passed through her mind that she might make some use of it herself. She held it up against herself.

'Now who's entering into temptation?' said Essy, glancing briefly at her, and delving back in the heap.

'It's just that it's in such good condition.'

'We'll get all the more for it,' cried Essy.

'It's extraordinary though,' said Mae. 'Things last so short a time now, and to think of how long this must have been here — I suppose it must have been our father's, or is that possible?'

Essy was surprised. She hardly remembered their father.

'There used to be uncles who came here in the old days,' she said, 'on visits.'

'They didn't leave much behind, though, as well as I remember,' said Mae. 'Very little we got out of anybody,' she said, with sudden bitterness, ' 'specially father's people. Let it go with the rest,' she said, with sudden vindictiveness. 'And now to get hold of a second-hand dealer!'

'That's easy,' cried Essy, and Mae could only marvel

at the way she had entered into the spirit of the thing, when she had at last got rid of her scruples. 'I'll run down the street,' she said. 'I know the very man.'

And in a few minutes she was back, flushed and triumphant.

'He'll call right away,' she said. 'They'll be auctioned this afternoon! I think that is a good thing somehow.'

'We'd hardly change our mind,' said Mae, but she knew well what Essy meant.

With all their differences, they weren't sisters for nothing, and she knew *just* how Essy felt. All those things, the coats and the blazers and poor mother's black things, and the bit of marabout — all of them were like a little family : a covey, a nest of things. They had been parted from their home; the place where they had huddled together warmly, for so long, but they still had each other! Soon they would be scattered on the four winds.

'At least we'll have the money right away!' she said, practicality returning, as the sound of van-wheels caught her ear.

'Try to lower your voice, Essy,' she said. 'It's as well for Charlie not to know anything about this. People don't understand other people. And ask the man when we'll be paid : that's very important.' It was better for Essy to conduct the transaction.

'He'll leave in the money on his way home to his tea,' Essy whispered, after she closed the door. 'He was very kind,' she added.

The money, when it was handed in that evening, was, however, extraordinarily little.

'Is that *all*?' cried Mae. 'He mustn't have sold all of the things; that gaberdine coat, for instance, the one I was so anxious to keep, that ought to have made two-pounds-ten alone, without all the rest.'

For that was all they got for the lot : two-pounds-ten.

'Well, it's better than nothing.' said Essy.

'Lower your voice, Essy,' said Mae. Charlie was still in the house, working late.

They were still standing at the door, the money in Essy's hand.

'I think we're going to have more frost,' said Essy.

'Well, we've more to think of than the weather,' said Mae, closing the door. 'I wish in a way that Charlie was working regular hours — union hours —' Because they didn't feel like getting ready a meal, a proper meal, till he was gone.

At last, however, Charlie gave up for the night.

'It's the cold that put a stop to me,' he said. 'Handling paper is a cold job.' He was in the hall, wiping paste off his hands. 'I'm glad I brought my muffler, I didn't wear it coming this morning, but you never know when it's going to change, and I stuffed it into the pocket of my coat.'

He lifted up an end of the plush curtain that was still in a heap on the floor, and dragged it out from the wall.

'Did you hang the things up?' he said then, looking around, and in particular and with some surprise at the empty rack. 'I put it on top of a heap of old clothes,' he said.

And then, for all the door having been closed, and their having whispered, and for all his ceaseless whistling, Charlie hadn't missed much. Before they knew themselves what had happened, he knew.

'You didn't sell it with your poor mother's things, did you?' he said.

Mae put her hand to her mouth. Then, as he looked so menacingly at her, she stepped back against the wall.

She wanted to say she'd replace it, but she felt a cautious instinct to say nothing.

'It'll have to be replaced, that's all,' said Charlie, 'and that won't be easy. Coats like that aren't readily got:

lined throughout it was, and double lining across the back.'

'How much was it worth?' said Mae at last.

'Oh, that's not the point at all,' said Charlie. 'It's what I paid for it that counts.'

'You didn't get it all that recently!' said Mae, in a small flash of defiance.

'That wouldn't be any concern to a judge and jury,' said Charlie. 'That coat will set you back a cool nine quid; do you hear that?'

They heard it all right, or at least Mae heard it. You'd think Essy didn't realize their position at all.

'You'll have to put sacking over your shoulders to-night anyway, Charlie,' she said. 'You can't go home like that. It's freezing outside. And we'll do something about the coat. Things always work themselves out in the end.'

It was such a bold front that Charlie was vanquished.

'I'll be coming to finish the parlour anyway,' he said, as if accepting the truce for the moment.

But when he was gone, Mae sat down there in the hall, on the plush curtain.

'It's all very well to say we'll do something, but what will we do?' she cried.

'Don't let's worry just yet,' said Essy. 'Things are never so bad they can't be worse, I say. It will be all the same in a hundred years' time.'

To think I pitied her for not being free, thought Mae, looking at her, for it was clear that with all her notions and nonsense, Essy's mind was like a faery cavern, with chamber after chamber opening one out of the other. Whereas she, Mae, was the one that was trapped. She was the responsible one. And what was she to do?

'Could you wire to Tom for some money?' said Essy.

'Is it to *him*?' cried Mae. It was no time to make bones of her relationship with her husband. 'I'd rather die than ask him,' she cried. 'I kept track of every penny I spent. I was determined he wouldn't be at a penny loss; except for the fare. You see, he expected he'd be asked for something: he was prepared to pay up!' The tears began to fill her eyes. 'I'd rather stay here than do that,' she cried.

'Well, why don't you?' cried Essy, and she giggled. Mae looked at her through tears.

'I wish to God I was like you, Essy!' she said, but if this was meant in malice and spite, it failed of its purpose.

'I never saw you cry before, Mae,' said Essy. 'Not since we were children, I mean,' she said politely, and with a great wish to be exact and proper.

In a Cafe

THE café was in a back street. Mary's ankles ached and she was glad Maudie had not got there before her. She sat down at a table near the door.

It was a place she had only recently found, and she dropped in often, whenever she came up to Dublin. She hated to go anywhere else now. For one thing, she knew that she would be unlikely ever to have set foot in it if Richard were still alive. And this knowledge helped to give her back a semblance of the identity she lost willingly in marriage, but lost doubly, and unwillingly, in widowhood.

Not that Richard would have disliked the café. It was the kind of place they went to when they were students. Too much water had gone under the bridge since those days, though. Say what you liked, there was something faintly snobby about a farm in Meath, and together she and Richard would have been out of place here. But it was a different matter to come here alone. There could be nothing — oh, nothing — snobby about a widow. Just by being one, she fitted into this kind of café. It was an unusual little place. She looked around.

The walls were distempered red above and the lower part was boarded, with the boards painted white. It was probably the boarded walls that gave it the peculiarly functional look you get in the snuggery of a public-house or in the confessional of a small and poor parish church. For furniture there were only deal tables and chairs, with black-and-white checked tablecloths that were either unironed or badly ironed. But there was a decided feeling that money was not so much in short supply as dedicated to other purposes — as witness the paintings on the walls, and a notice over the fire-grate to say that there were others on view in a studio overhead, in rather the same way as pictures in an exhibition. They were for the most part experimental in their technique.

The café was run by two students from the Art College. They often went out and left the place quite empty — as now — while they had a cup of coffee in another café — across the street. Regular clients sometimes helped themselves to coffee from the pot on the gas-ring, behind a curtain at the back ; or, if they only came in for company and found none, merely warmed themselves at the big fire always blazing in the little black grate that was the original grate when the café was a warehouse office. Today, the fire was banked up with coke. The coffee was spitting on the gas-ring.

Would Maudie like the place ? That it might not be exactly the right place to have arranged to meet her, above all under the present circumstances, occurred vaguely to Mary, but there was nothing that could be done about it now. When Maudie got there, if she didn't like it, they could go somewhere else. On the other hand, perhaps she might like it ? Or perhaps she would be too upset to take notice of her surroundings ? The paintings might interest her. They were certainly stimulating. There were two new ones today, which Mary herself had not seen before : two flower paintings, just inside the door. From where she sat she could read the signature, Johann van Stiegler. Or at least they suggested flowers. They were nameable as roses surely in spite of being a bit angular. She knew what Richard would have said about them. But she and Richard were no longer one. So what would *she* say about them ? She would say — she would say —

But what was keeping Maudie ? It was all very well to

be glad of a few minutes' time in which to gather herself
together; it was a different thing altogether to be kept
a quarter of an hour.

Mary leaned back against the boarding. She was less
tired than when she came in, but she was still in no way
prepared for the encounter in front of her.

What had she to say to a young widow recently be-
reaved? Why on earth had she arranged to meet her?
The incongruity of their both being widowed came for-
cibly upon her. Would Maudie, too, be in black with
touches of white? Two widows! It was like two mag-
pies : one for sorrow, two for joy. The absurdity of it
was all at once so great she had an impulse to get up and
make off out of the place. She felt herself vibrating all
over with resentment at being coupled with anyone, and
urgently she began to sever them, seeking out their disparities.

Maudie was only a year married! And her parents
had been only too ready to take care of her child, greedily
possessing themselves of it. Maudie was as free as a girl.
Then — if it mattered — ? — she had a nice little income
in her own right too, apart from all Michael had left her.
So?

But what was keeping her? Was she not coming at
all?

Ah! the little iron bell that was over the door — it
too, since the warehouse days — tinkled to tell there was
another customer coming into the café.

It wasn't Maudie though. It was a young man —
youngish anyway — and Mary would say that he was an
artist. Yet his hands at which, when he sat down, he
began to stare, were not like the hands of an artist. They
were peculiarly plump soft-skinned hands, and there was
something touching in the relaxed way in which, lightly
clasped one in the other, they rested on the table. Had
they a womanish look perhaps? No; that was not the

word, but she couldn't for the life of her find the right word to describe them. And her mind was teased by trying to find it. Fascinated, her eyes were drawn to those hands, time and again, no matter how resolutely she tore them away. It was almost as if it was by touch, not sight, that she knew their warm fleshiness.

Even when she closed her eyes — as she did — she could still see them. And so, innocent of where she was being led, she made no real effort to free her thoughts from them, and not until it was too late did she see before her the familiar shape of her recurring nightmare. All at once it was Richard's hands she saw, so different from those others, wiry, supple, thin. There they were for an instant in her mind, limned by love and anguish, before they vanished.

It happened so often. In her mind she would see a part of him, his hand — his arm, his foot perhaps, in the finely worked leather shoes he always wore — and from it, frantically, she would try to build up the whole man. Sometimes she succeeded better than others, built him up from foot to shoulder, seeing his hands, his grey suit, his tie, knotted always in a slightly special way, his neck, even his chin that was rather sharp, a little less attractive than his other features —

— But always at that point she would be defeated. Never once voluntarily since the day he died had she been able to see his face again.

And if she could not remember him, at will, what meaning had time at all? What use was it to have lived the past, if behind us it fell away so sheer?

In the hour of his death, for her it was part of the pain that she knew this would happen. She was standing beside him when, outside the hospital window, a bird called out with a sweet, clear whistle, and hearing it she knew that he was dead, because not for years had she really heard bird-song or bird-call, so loud was the noise of their

love in her ears. When she looked down it was a strange
face, the look of death itself, that lay on the pillow. And
after that brief moment of silence that let in the bird-song
for an instant, a new noise started in her head; the noise
of a nameless panic that did not always roar, but never
altogether died down.

And now — here in the little café — she caught at the
table-edge — for the conflagration had started again and
her mind was a roaring furnace.

It was just then the man at the end of the table stood
up and reached for the menu-card on which, as a matter
of fact, she was leaning — breasts and elbows — with her
face in her hands. Hastily, apologetically, she pushed it
towards him, and at once the roar died down in her mind.
She looked at him. Could he have known? Her heart
was filled with gratitude, and she saw that his eyes were
soft and gentle. But she had to admit that he didn't look
as if he were much aware of her. No matter! She still
was grateful to him.

'Don't you want this too?' she cried, thankful, warm,
as she saw that the small small slip of paper with the
speciality for the day that had been clipped to the menu
card with a paper-pin, had come off and remained under
her elbow, caught on the rough sleeve of her jacket. She
stood up and leant over the table with it.

'Ah! thank you!' he said, and bowed. She smiled.
There was such gallantry in a bow. He was a foreigner,
of course. And then, before she sat down again she saw
that he had been sketching, making little pencil sketches
all over a newspaper on the table, in the margins and in
the spaces between the newsprint. Such intricate minutely
involuted little figures — she was fascinated, but of course
she could not stare.

Yet, when she sat down, she watched him covertly, and
every now and then she saw that he made a particular
flourish: it was his signature, she felt sure, and she tried

to make it out from where she sat. A disproportionate,
a ridiculous excitement rushed through her, when she
realised it was Johann van Stiegler, the name on the
new flower paintings that had preoccupied her when she
first came into the place.

But it's impossible, she thought. The sketches were
so meticulous; the paintings so —

But the little bell had tinkled again.

'Ah! Maudie!'

For all her waiting, taken by surprise in the end, she
got to her feet in her embarrassment, like a man.

'Maudie, my dear!' She had to stare fixedly at her
in an effort to convey the sympathy, which, tongue-tied,
she could express in no other way.

They shook hands, wordlessly.

'I'm deliberately refraining from expressing sympathy
— you know that?' said Mary then, as they sat down at
the checkered table.

'Oh, I do!' cried Maudie. And she seemed genuinely
appreciative. 'It's so awful trying to think of something
to say back! — Isn't it? It has to come right out of yourself, and sometimes what comes is something you can't
even say out loud when you do think of it!'

It was so true. Mary looked at her in surprise. Her
mind ran back over the things people had said to her,
and the replies.

Them: It's a good thing it wasn't one of the children.

Her: I'd give them all for him.

Them: Time is a great healer.

Her: Thief would be more like: taking away even my
    memory of him.

Them: God's ways are wonderful. Some day you'll
    see His plan in all this.

Her: Do you mean, some day I'll be glad he's dead?'

So Maudie apprehended these subtleties too? Mary
looked hard at her. 'I know, I know,' she said. 'In the

end you have to say what is expected of you — and you feel so cheapened by it.'

'Worse still, you cheapen the dead!' said Maudie.

Mary looked really hard at her now. Was it possible for a young girl — a simple person at that — to have wrung from one single experience so much bitter knowledge? In spite of herself, she felt she was being drawn into complicity with her. She drew back resolutely.

'Of course, you were more or less expecting it, weren't you?' she said, spitefully.

Unrepulsed, Maudie looked back at her. 'Does that matter?' she asked, and then, unexpectedly, she herself put a rift between them. 'You have the children, of course!' she said, and then, hastily, before Mary could say anything, she rushed on. 'Oh, I know I have my baby, but there seems so little link between him and his father! I just can't believe that it's me, sometimes, wheeling him round the park in his pram: it's like as if he was illegitimate. No! I mean it really. I'm not just trying to be shocking. It must be so different when there has been time for a relationship to be started between children and their father, like there was in your case.'

'Oh, I don't know that that matters,' said Mary. 'And you'll be glad to have him some day.' This time she spoke with deliberate malice, for she knew so well how those same words had lacerated her. She knew what they were meant to say: the children would be better than nothing.

But the poison of her words did not penetrate Maudie. And with another stab she knew why this was so. Maudie was so young; so beautiful. Looking at her, it seemed quite inaccurate to say that she had lost her husband: it was Michael who had lost her, fallen out, as it were, while she perforce went outward. She didn't even look like a widow. There was nothing about her to suggest that she was in any way bereft or maimed.

'You'll marry again, Maudie,' she said, impulsively. 'Don't mind my saying it,' she added quickly, hastily. 'It's not a criticism. It's because I know how you're suffering that I say it. Don't take offence.'

Maudie didn't really look offended though, she only looked on the defensive. Then she relaxed.

'Not coming from you,' she said. 'You know what it's like.' Mary saw she was trying to cover up the fact that she simply could not violently refute the suggestion. 'Not that I think I will,' she added, but weakly. 'After all, you didn't !'

It was Mary who was put upon the defensive now.

'After all, it's only two years — less even,' she said stiffly.

'Oh, it's not altogether a matter of time,' said Maudie, seeing she had erred, but not clear how or where. 'It's the kind of person you are, I think. I admire you so much ! It's what I'd want to be like myself if I had the strength. With remarriage it is largely the effect on one-self that matters I think, don't you ? I don't think it really matters to — to the dead ! Do you ? I'm sure Michael would want me to marry again if he were able to express a wish. After all, people say it's a compliment to a man if his widow marries again, did you ever hear that ?'

'I did,' said Mary, curtly. 'But I wouldn't pay much heed to it. A fat lot of good the dead care about compliments.'

So Maudie *was* already thinking about remarriage ? Mary's irritation was succeeded by a vague feeling of envy, and then the irritation returned tenfold.

How easily it was accepted that *she* would not marry again. This girl regards me as too old, of course. And she's right — or she ought to be right ! She remembered the way, even two years ago, people had said she "had" her children. They meant, even then, that it was un-likely, unlooked for, that she'd remarry.

Other things that had been said crowded back into her mind as well. So many people had spoken of the special quality of her marriage — her's and Richard's — their remarkable suitability one for the other, and the uniqueness of the bond between them. She was avid to hear this said at the time.

But suddenly, in this little café, the light that had played over those words, flickered and went out. Did they perhaps mean that if Richard had not appeared when he did, no one else would have been interested in her?

Whereas Maudie — ! If she looked so attractive now, when she must still be suffering from shock, what would she be like a year from now, when she would be "out of mourning," as it would be put? Why, right now, she was so fresh and — looking at her there was no other word for it — virginal! Of course she was only a year married. A year! You could hardly call it being married at all.

But Maudie knew a thing or two about men for all that. There was no denying it. And in her eyes at that moment there was a strange expression. Seeing it, Mary remembered at once that they were not alone in the café. She wondered urgently how much the man at the other end of the table had heard and could hear of what they were saying. But it was too late to stop Maudie.

'Oh Mary,' cried Maudie, leaning forward, 'it's not what they give us — I've got over wanting things like a child — it's what we have to give them! It's something——' and she pressed her hands suddenly to her breasts, 'something in here!'

'Maudie!'

Sharply, urgently, Mary tried to make her lower her voice, and with a quick movement of her head she did manage at last to convey some caution to her.

'In case you might say something,' she said, in a low voice.

'Oh, there was no fear,' said Maudie. 'I was aware all the time.' She didn't speak quite so low as Mary, but did lower her voice. 'I was aware of him *all the time*,' she said. 'It was *him* that put it into my mind — about what we have to give.' She pressed her hands to her breasts again. 'He looks so lonely, don't you think? He is a foreigner, isn't he? I always think it's sad for them; they don't have many friends, and even when they do, there is always a barrier, don't you agree?'

But Mary was too embarrassed to let her go on. Almost frantically she made a diversion.

'What are you going to have, Maudie?' she said, loudly. 'Coffee? Tea? And is there no one to take an order?'

Immediately she felt a fool. To whom had she spoken? She looked across at Johann van Stiegler. As if he were waiting to meet her glance, his mild and patient eyes looked into her's.

'There is no one there,' he said, nodding at the curtained gas-ring, 'but one can serve oneself. Perhaps you would wish that I——'

'Oh not at all,' cried Mary. 'Please don't trouble! We're in absolutely no hurry! Please don't trouble yourself,' she said, 'not on our account.'

But she saw at once that he was very much a foreigner, and that he was at a disadvantage, not knowing if he had not perhaps made a gaffe. 'I have perhaps intruded?' he said, miserably.

'Oh, not at all,' cried Mary, and he was so serious she had to laugh.

The laugh was another mistake though. His face took on a look of despair that could come upon a foreigner, it seemed, at the slightest provocation, as if suddenly everything was obscure to him — everything.

'Please,' she murmured, and then vaguely, '— your work,' meaning that she did not wish to interrupt his sketching.

'Ah, you know my work?' he said, brightening immediately, pleased and with a small and quite endearing vanity. 'We have met before? Yes?'

'Oh no, we haven't met,' she said, quickly, and she sat down, but of course after that it was impossible to go on acting as if he were a complete stranger. She turned to see what Maudie would make of the situation. It was then she felt the full force of her irritation with Maudie. She could have given her a slap in the face. Yes: a slap right in the face! For there she sat, remotely, her face indeed partly averted from them.

Maudie was waiting to be introduced! To be *introduced*, as if she, Mary, did not need any conventional preliminaries. As if it was all right that she, Mary, should begin an unprefaced conversation with a strange man in a café because — and of course that was what was so infuriating, that she knew Maudie's unconscious thought — it was all right for a woman of *her* age to strike up a conversation like that, but that it wouldn't have done for a young woman. Yet, on her still partly averted face, Mary could see the quickened look of interest. She had a good mind not to make any gesture to draw her into the conversation at all, but she had the young man to consider. She had to bring them together whether she liked it or not.

'Maudie, this is—' she turned back and smiled at van Stiegler, 'this is—' But she was confused and she had to abandon the introduction altogether. Instead, she broke into a direct question.

'Those are your flower pictures, aren't they?' she asked.

It was enough for Maudie — more than enough you might say.

She turned to the young man, obviously greatly impressed; her lips apart, her eyes shining. My God, how attractive she was!

'Oh no, not really?' she cried. 'How marvellous of you!'

But Johann van Stiegler was looking at Mary.

'You are sure we have not met before?'

'Oh no, but you were scribbling your signature all over that newspaper,' she looked around to show it to him, but it had fallen on to the floor.

'Ah yes,' he said, and — she couldn't be certain, of course — but she thought he was disappointed.

'Ah yes, you saw my signature,' he said, flatly. He looked dejected. Mary felt helpless. She turned to Maudie. It was up to her to say something now.

Just then the little warehouse bell tinkled again, and this time it was one of the proprietors who came in, casually, like a client.

'Ah good!' said van Stiegler. 'Coffee,' he called out. Then he turned to Mary. 'Coffee for you too?'

'Oh yes, coffee for us,' said Mary, but she couldn't help wondering who was going to pay for it, and simultaneously she couldn't help noticing the shabbiness of his jacket. Well — they'd see! Meanwhile, she determined to ignore the plate of cakes that was put down with the coffee. And she hoped Maudie would too. She pushed the plate aside as a kind of hint to her, but Maudie leaned across and took a large bun filled with cream.

'Do you mind my asking you something — about your work—?' said Mary.

But Maudie interrupted.

'You are living in Ireland? I mean, you are not just here on a visit?'

There was intimacy and intimacy, and Mary felt nervous in case the young man might resent this question.

'I teach art in a college here,' he said, and he did seem a little surprised, but Mary could see too, that he was not at all displeased. He seemed to settle more comfortably into the conversation.

'It is very good for a while to go to another country,' he said, 'and this country is cheap. I have a flat in the next street to here, and it is very private. If I hang myself from the ceiling, it is all right — nobody knows; nobody cares. That is a good way to live when you paint.'

Mary was prepared to ponder. 'Do you think so?'

Maudie was not prepared to ponder. 'How odd,' she said, shortly, and then she looked at her watch. 'I'll have to go,' she said, inexplicably.

They had finished the coffee. Immediately Mary's thoughts returned to the problem of who was to pay for it. It was a small affair for which to call up all one's spiritual resources, but she felt enormously courageous and determined when she heard herself ask in a loud voice for her bill.

'My bill, please,' she called out, over the sound of spitting coffee on the gas stove.

Johann van Stiegler made no move to ask for his bill, and yet he was buttoning his jacket and folding his newspaper as if to leave too. Would his coffee go on her bill? Mary wondered.

It was all settled, however, in a second. The bill was for two eight-penny coffees, and one bun, and there was no charge for van Stiegler's coffee. He had some understanding with the owners, she supposed. Or perhaps he was not really going to leave then at all?

As they stood up, however, gloved and ready to depart, the young man bowed.

'Perhaps we go the same way?' and they could see he was anxious to be polite.

'Oh, not at all,' they said together, as if he had offered to escort them, and Maudie even laughed openly.

Then there was, of course, another ridiculous situation. van Stiegler sat down again. Had they been too brusque? Had they hurt his feelings?

Oh, if only he wasn't a foreigner, thought Mary, and

she hesitated. Maudie already had her hand on the door.

'I hope I will see some more of your work sometime,' said Mary. It was not a question, merely a compliment.

But van Stiegler sprung to his feet again though.

'Tonight after my classes I am bringing another picture to hang here,' he said. 'You would like to see it? I would be here—' he pulled out a large, old-fashioned watch, '— at ten minutes past nine.'

'Oh, not tonight — I couldn't come back tonight,' said Mary. 'I live in the country, you see,' she said, explaining and excusing herself. 'Another time perhaps? It will be here for how long?'

She wasn't really listening to what he said. She was thinking that he had not asked if Maudie could come. Perhaps it was that, of the two of them, she looked the most likely to buy a picture, whereas Maudie, although in actual fact more likely to do so, looked less so. Or was it that he coupled them so that he thought if one came, both came. Or was it really Maudie he'd like to see again, and that he regarded her as a chaperone? Or was it—?

There was no knowing, however, and so she said goodbye again, and the next minute the little bell had tinkled over the door and they were in the street. In the street they looked at each other.

'Well! if ever there was—' began Maudie, but she didn't get time to finish her sentence. Behind them the little bell tinkled yet again, and their painter was out in the street with them.

'I forgot to give you the address of my flat — it is also my studio,' he said. 'I would be glad to show you my paintings at any time.' He pulled out a notebook and tore out a sheet. 'I will write it down,' he said, concisely. And he did. But when he went to hand it to them, it was Maudie who took it. 'I am nearly always there, except when I am at my classes,' he said. And bowing, he turned and went back into the café.

They dared not laugh until they had walked some distance away, until they turned into the next street in fact.

'Well, I never!' said Maudie, and she handed the paper to Mary.

'Chatham Row,' Mary read, 'number 8.'

'Will you go to see them?' asked Maudie.

Mary felt outraged.

'What do you take me for?' she asked. 'I may be a bit unconventional, but can you see me presenting myself at his place? Would *you* go?'

'Oh, it's different for me,' said Maudie, enigmatically. 'And anyway, it was you he asked. But I see your point — it's a pity. Poor fellow! — he must be very lonely. I wish there was something we could do for him — some-one to whom we could introduce him.'

Mary looked at her. It had never occurred to her that he might be lonely! How was it that the obvious always escaped her?

They were in Grafton Street by this time.

'Well, I have some shopping to do. I suppose it's the same with you,' said Maudie. 'I am glad I had that talk with you. We must have another chat soon.'

'Oh yes,' said Mary, over-readily, replying to their adieux though, and not as Maudie thought, to the sugges-tion of their meeting again! She was anxious all at once to be rid of Maudie.

And yet, as she watched her walk away from her, making her passage quickly and expertly through the crowds in the street, Mary felt a sudden terrible aimless-ness descend upon herself like a physical paralysis. She walked along, passing to look in at the shop windows.

It was the evening hour when everyone in the streets was hurrying home, purposeful and intent. Even those who paused to look into the shop windows did so with direction and aim, darting their bright glances keenly, like birds. Their minds were all intent upon substantives;

tangibles, while her mind was straying back to the student café, and the strange flower pictures on the walls; to the young man who was so vulnerable in his vanity: the legitimate vanity of his art.

It was so like Maudie to laugh at him. What did she know of an artist's mind? If Maudie had not been with her, it would have been so different. She might, for one thing, have got him to talk about his work, to explain the discrepancy between the loose style of the pictures on the wall and the exact, small sketches he'd been drawing on the margins of the paper.

She might even have taken up his invitation to go and see his paintings. Why had that seemed so unconventional — so laughable? Because of Maudie, that was why.

How ridiculous their scruples would have seemed to the young man. She could only hope he had not guessed them. She looked up at a clock. Supposing, right now, she were to slip back to the café and suggest that after all she found she would have time for a quick visit to his studio? Or would he have left the café? Better perhaps to call around to the studio? He would surely be back there now!

For a moment she stood debating the arguments for and against going back. Would it seem odd to him? Would he be surprised? But as if it were Maudie who put the questions, she frowned them down and all at once purposeful as anyone in the street, began to go back, headlong, you might say, towards Chatham Street.

At the point where two small streets crossed each other she had to pause, while a team of Guinness's dray horses turned with difficulty in the narrow cube of the intersection. And, while she waited impatiently, she caught sight of herself in the gilded mirror of a public-house. For a second, the familiar sight gave her a misgiving of her mission, but as the dray-horses moved out of the way, she told herself that her dowdy, lumpish, and unromantic figure vouched for her spiritual integrity. She pulled herself away from the face in the glass and hurried across the street.

Between two lock-up shops, down a short alley — roofed by the second storey of the premises overhead, till it was like a tunnel — was his door. Away at the end of the tunnel the door could clearly be seen even from the middle of the street, for it was painted bright yellow. Odd that she had never seen it in the times she had passed that way. She crossed the street.

Once across the street, she ran down the tunnel, her footsteps echoing loud in her ears. And there on the door, tied to the latchet of the letter-box, was a piece of white cardboard with his name on it. Grabbing the knocker, she gave three clear hammer-strokes on the door.

The little alley was a sort of cul-de-sac; except for the street behind her and the door in front of her, it had no outlet. There was not even a skylight or an aperture of any kind. As for the premises into which the door led, there was no way of telling its size or its extent, or anything at all about it, until the door was opened.

Irresponsibly, she giggled. It was like the mystifying doors in the trunks of trees that beguiled her as a child in fairy-tales and fantasies. Did this door, too, like those fairy doors, lead into rooms of impossible amplitude, or would it be a cramped and poky place?

As she pondered upon what was within, seemingly so mysteriously sealed, she saw that — just as in a fairy tale — after all there was an aperture. The letter-box had lost its shutter, or lid, and it gaped open, a vacant hole in the wood, reminding her of a sleeping doll whose eye-balls had been poked back in its head, and creating an expression of vacancy and emptiness.

Impulsively, going down on one knee, she peered in through the slit.

At first she could see only segments of the objects within, but by moving her head, she was able to identify things: an unfinished canvas up against the splattered white wainscot, a bicycle-pump flat on the floor, the leg of a table, black iron bed-legs and, to her amusement, dangling down by the leg of the table, dripping their moisture in a pool on the floor, a pair of elongated, grey, wool socks. It was, of course, only possible to see the lower portion of the room, but it seemed enough to infer conclusively that this was indeed a little room in a tree, no bigger than the bulk of the outer trunk, leading no-where, and — sufficient or no — itself its own end.

There was just one break in the wainscot, where a door ran down to the floor, but this was so narrow and made of roughly-jointed boards, that she took it to be the door of a press. And then, as she started moving, she saw something else, an intricate segment of fine wire spokes. It was a second before she realised it was the wheel of a bicycle.

So, a bicycle, too, lived here, in this little room in a tree-trunk!

Oh, poor young man, poor painter: poor foreigner, inept at finding the good lodgings in a strange city. Her heart went out to him.

It was just then that the boarded door — it couldn't have been a press after all — opened into the room, and she found herself staring at two feet. They were large feet, shoved into unlaced shoes, and they were bare to the white ankles. For, of course, she thought wildly, focusing her thoughts, his socks are washed! But her power to think clearly only lasted an instant. She sprang to her feet.

'Who iss that?' asked a voice. 'Did someone knock?'

It was the voice of the man in the café. But where was she to find a voice with which to reply? And who was she to say what she was? Who — to this stranger — was she?

And if he opened the door, what then? All the thoughts and words that had, like a wind, blown her down this tunnel, subsided suddenly, and she stood, appalled, at where they had brought her.

'Who iss that?' came the voice within, troubled.

Staring at those white feet, thrust into the unlaced shoes, she felt that she would die on the spot if they moved an inch. She turned.

Ahead of her, bright, shining and clear, as if it were at the end of a powerful telescope, was the street. Not caring if her feet were heard, volleying and echoing as if she ran through a mighty drain-pipe, she kept running till she reached the street, kept running even then, jostling surprised shoppers, hitting her ankles off the wheel-knobs of push-cars and prams. Only when she came to the junction of the streets again, did she stop, as in the pub mirror she caught sight again of her familiar face. That face steadied her. How absurd to think that anyone would sinisterly follow this middle-aged woman?

But suppose he had been in the outer room when she knocked! If he had opened the door? What would have happened then? What would she have said? A flush spread over her face. The only true words that she could have uttered were those that had sunk into her mind in the café; put there by Maudie.

'I'm lonely!' That was all she could have said. 'I'm lonely. Are you?'

A deep shame came over her with this admission and, guiltily, she began to walk quickly onward again, towards Grafton Street. If anyone had seen her, there in that dark alleyway! If anyone could have looked into her mind, her heart!

And yet, was it so unnatural? Was it so hard to understand? So unforgiveable?

As she passed the open door of the Carmelite Church she paused. Could she rid herself of her feeling of shame

in the dark of the confessional? To the sin-accustomed
ears of the wise old fathers her story would be light-weight;
a tedious tale of scrupulosity. Was there no one, no one
who'd understand?

She had reached Grafton Street once more, and
stepped into its crowded thoroughfare. It was only a few
minutes since she left it, but in the street the evasion of
light had begun. Only the bustle of people, and the
activity of traffic, made it seem that it was yet day. Away
at the top of the street, in Stephen's Green, to which she
turned, although the tops of the trees were still clear,
branch for branch, in the last of the light, mist muted
the outline of the bushes. If one were to put a hand between the railings now, it would be with a slight shock
that the fingers would feel the little branches, like fine
bones, under the feathers of mist. And in their secret
nests the smaller birds were making faint avowals in the
last of the day. It was the time at which she used to meet
Richard.

Oh Richard! she cried, almost out loud, as she walked
along by the railings to where the car was parked. Oh
Richard! it's you I want.

And as she cried out, her mind presented him to her,
as she so often saw him, coming towards her: tall, hand-
some, and with his curious air of apartness from those
around him. He had his hat in his hand, down by his
side, as on a summer day he might trail a hand in water
from the side of a boat. She wanted to preserve that
picture of him forever in an image, and only as she
struggled to hold on to it did she realize there was
no urgency in the search. She had a sense of having all
the time in the world to look and look and look at him.
That was the very way he used to come to meet her —
indolently trailing the old felt hat, glad to be done with
the day; and when they got nearer to each other she
used to take such joy in his unsmiling face, with its

happiness integral to it in all its features. It was the first time in the two years he'd been gone from her that she'd seen his face.

Not till she had taken out the key of the car, and gone straight around to the driver's side, not stupidly, as so often, to the passenger seat — not till then did she realize what she had achieved. Yet she had no more than got back her rights. No more. It was not a subject for amazement. By what means exactly had she got them back though — in that little café? That was the wonder.

Lemonade

It couldn't last. Not all the lemonade anyway.

'Like another bottle?' Uncle Pauddy asked.

'Take one any time you feel like it,' said Uncle Matt. He took her inside the counter and showed her how to use the bottle-opener.

She had a few bottles just for the pleasure of prising off the caps, but she was really sick of lemonade. To hear the uncles, you'd think she never got any till she came to Ireland. On the boat she got plenty. Back in Boston, Pappa's friends often treated her.

'Whatever about you, Dinny,' they'd say, 'we can't let the child go home thirsty!' Though in fairness to the Irish uncles, she had to admit there was no ambiguity about the lemonade in Ireland. In Boston she never knew whether Mama or Pappa meant real lemonade, or the kind Pappa drank. It was confusing, like the night before they sailed for Ireland.

All Pappa's and Mama's friends had come to the house to say good-bye, that is to say, all Pappa's friends. Mama didn't want them.

'On our last night!' she sighed, when Pappa announced they were coming.

'I know, I know,' said Pappa, 'only it wasn't me who asked them. They invited themselves — out of the goodness of their hearts!' he added.

'— or maybe,' cried Mama — 'as a cure for the drought!'

'Oh come now: don't be bitter on our last night,' said Pappa.

And so they came; all the old cronies. There was

barely room in the parlour for them all, especially with the trunks and boxes, strapped and corded with new white rope, in the middle of the floor, and on the top of one of the trunks, a big bunch of asters wrapped in wet newspaper.

'Don't sit on the asters, please!' Mama kept saying all evening.

'Wait a minute: wait a minute, boys,' cried Pappa, as the cronies came in the door, and he lifted up the red plush skirt that draped the table legs, and pulled out a crate. 'We can get rid of this box and make more room, if some of you give me a hand to empty out what's in it!'

Everybody laughed but Mama.

'Ah come now, ma'am,' said one of the cronies, and he pointed to the round tin seals, that were soldered to the twisted wire every place it was knotted. 'What harm can be in it, when it's covered with medals?'

Mama didn't heed him.

'Dinny, you gave me your solemn word —' she said.

'So I did! So I did!' cried Pappa,' — but it doesn't take effect till your ship sails, girlie! Come now, don't be a spoil-sport.'

The next minute the crate was split open, and Pappa ran into the kitchen and came back with a bunch of glasses, held by their stems like flowers.

'Now, who's for lemonade?' he cried. Then he bit his lip. 'Gee, honey,' he said, and he ran over to Maudie. 'Amn't I the bad Pappa. I forgot to get real lemonade for you.'

It was because he was so sad, not because she was disappointed — that the tears came into Maudie's eyes.

'There,' cried Mama, seeing the tears, 'I knew something like this would happen!'

But Maudie dashed the tears away.

'I don't mind, Mama!' she cried. She shook Pappa's shoulder. 'Honest I don't!'

'Don't you?' Pappa looked up at her. 'Honest, girlie?' The happy look came back to his face. He had only one girlie now to placate. 'How about giving the child a little drop of what we have — well diluted, of course — to make up to her?' he whispered to Mama.

Mama was almost speechless.

'Dinny Delaney! — it's when you say things like that that I know I am doing right in —'

But Pappa clapped his hand over her mouth, and he spoke very low, so that no one could hear but Maudie.

'No more of that!' he said. 'Tut-tut. A bargain is a bargain. A little holiday — that was what we agreed to call it — you needed it badly: if anyone ever deserved it, it's you, girl. A little holiday. No reasons asked and none given. Isn't that what we decided? And don't forget it when you get the other side either.' He looked very cross for a minute, and stared down into the drink in his glass. Then he raised his eyes. 'Indeed, a little nip wouldn't hurt you either — for health reasons,' he added, quickly. 'I'm telling you, you needn't look so stuck-up about it — and this time tomorrow you may be glad to remember my words — but the best preparation for a sea-voyage is a drop of this stuff here,' and he tapped the glass in his hand. 'I see you don't heed me, but I know what I'm talking about, and it was a bar-tender — wait! — what am I talking about, it wasn't a bar-tender at all but a steward on board ship, that told me himself about a young woman — just your own age — on one of his crossings — and she was so sick the ship's doctor thought it was all up with her, and so it might have been if it weren't for the steward's presence of mind in forcing a drop of drink down her throat. That's the truth I'm telling you, girl. And don't forget it either. And remember, if the child happens to get sick—' Here, he went to sit down again beside Maudie, but Mama gave a scream.

'Mind the asters!' she cried. 'Oh, they're ruined,' she said, snatching them up and examining them.

They were getting a bit tattered. A lot of raggy petals had come undone and littered the floor like scraps of knitting wool.

'I did so want to have them with us on the voyage,' Mama wailed.

'How many times have you made the voyage, ma'am?' asked one of the cronies politely.

'How many times did I cross the Atlantic, Dinny?' Mama asked, but she didn't wait for his answer. 'Four times,' she said, 'counting this time, of course,' she added, scrupulously.

'You're not the whole way across yet girl!' said Pappa. 'There's such a thing as icebergs, you know,' he said, and he turned and looked soberly towards his guests. 'For all our advances in science and the like, we haven't got rid of the icebergs yet.'

'What are icebergs?' asked Maudie.

'Oh, they're nothing at all,' said Pappa, hastily, 'and anyway, who knows, but your Mama might get homesick yet and change her mind at the last minute, and then you wouldn't be going away at all!'

'Oh, but I *want* to go,' cried Maudie. 'I've told everybody I'm going, the teachers in school and all!'

'So *you* want to leave me too, do you?' he said, and he stared deep down into his glass that was empty now.

'Oh, don't start that kind of thing with her — with a *child*,' cried Mama. 'Naturally she's looking forward to the excitement. And anyway, she knows — or she's been told rather — that you're coming over to take us back in the spring.'

'Yes: she's been told that, I know,' said Pappa gloomily. Why was his voice so peculiar though? And

why did Mama raise her own voice and scatter her words
to all sides.

'It will be Dinny's fourteenth crossing — when he
comes over for us,' she said.

They were all amazed.

'Fourteen times across The Pond!' cried old Pa
Spiddal, immeasurably impressed. His real name was not
Spiddal at all. That was the name of the place he came
from back in Ireland. He talked about it so much that
he was never called anything else.

'That's true,' said Pappa, taking up again. 'And by
rights, some of them crossings ought to count double
because the crossings nowadays are not to be compared
with the crossings when I first came out here — Oh, those
early crossings! Did I ever tell you about the time——'

'I'm sure you did!' said Mama, hastily, but the others
were greedy for it.

They were all Irish, but not born-Irish, and so taking
part in this leave-taking of Dinny's wife and child had a
two-fold nostalgia for them, a nostalgia for the old
country, but also for the old people, now dead and gone,
through whose eyes, only, they had ever seen that lost land.

'Well,' said Dinny, ignoring Mama, '— to give you
an idea of the way we used to be tossed about in those
days, I must tell you there used to be a rim around the
tables to prevent the cups and saucers from sliding off on
to the floor — No! wait a minute. I think that must
have been on later crossings altogether — in the real
early days, when I was a young lad making my first
voyage — the cups and saucers were chained to the
tables — they were enamel cups, of course, or tin maybe
— but——'

'Dinny!' Mama's cheeks were blazing. 'Surely that
was only in steerage!' she cried.

'Yes — sure — it was steerage,' said Pappa, unem-
barrassed, and quite unaware of Mama's flushed face. 'I

don't know what it was like in first class,' he said, 'although as I used to say in those days, there wouldn't be much differ if the ship went down!'

But although one or two of the old cronies laughed, Maudie could see that one or two of the women had caught each other's eyes. And just then, she felt a stealthy movement down near her feet, that dangled over the edge of the trunk, and looking down — stealthily too — she saw that old Ma Spiddal had reached out her foot, and, with the tip of her black buttoned boot, was gently, but persuasively, pushing apart the two big steamer trunks.

But Mama saw it too. She snatched up the asters.

'Is it the labels you want to see, Ma Spiddal?' she asked, crisply. 'Not but that steerage nowadays is nearly as good as first class in the old days,' she said, showing — no — forcing the labels under Ma Spiddal's nose, 'still, it's not worth our while looking into a few dollars here or there, like as if we were emigrants!'

'Ah, it's more than a few dollars difference, my dear,' said Ma Spiddal, with a mixture of grudgingness, envy, but above all, contrition.

'Well, it's Dinny's concern anyway, not mine,' said Mama more gently. She looked down with some surprise at the asters in her hand. 'I'd better put these in water!'

'Water!' Pappa shuddered violently, — 'a sacrilegious word on this night,' he said, and he dived into the crate again to bring up another bunch of bottles.

But Mama whispered something to him, and next minute Maudie felt herself picked up bodily in Pappa's arms. And all the way up the stairs her head bobbed from side to side.

'Am I on the boat?' she cried. 'Is it sinking?'

'You see!' cried Mama to Pappa. 'I hope you're satisfied now with your old guffage! A nice time I'll have with her on the boat!'

'Well, I declare to God,' cried Pappa, 'anyone would

think to hear you that it was my idea for you to go instead of——'

'Instead of what?' flashed Mama.

'Oh what's the use going into it now,' said Pappa, and
he rummaged in his pocket. 'Here,' he said. 'I may as
well give you the tickets now.'

Mama took them and looked at them.

'Single fare?'

'You'll feel freer that way,' said Pappa.

'We'll lose money by not getting a return.'

'Only if you come back,' said Pappa, queerly.

Sleepy as she was, those words went through Maudie's
heart. And Pappa saw.

'Who knows, girlie? I may go over and settle down
there myself,' he said, jocularly, but the jocularity didn't
satisfy even him. 'Give me back those tickets for a minute,'
He whipped out a pencil from his pocket and put a
little cross on the back of one of the tickets. 'That
stands for lemonade,' he said to Maudie. 'Show it to the
steward on the boat and he'll understand. It's my mark.
It means I'll pay for it when I go across next time —
Mama will arrange things if there's any difficulty.'

Mama snatched back the tickets, in no way pleased,
though.

'Can we never discuss anything seriously?' she said.
'Isn't it decided that you're coming over in March to
bring us back?'

'That was the idea at the start,' said Pappa.

'Well?' said Mama.

'Well!' said Pappa. 'Oh, I'll go over all right,' he
said, slowly, 'but who knows if we mightn't all settle down
over there.

Mama looked dubious.

'You mightn't find the company so much to your
liking over there.'

'Oh, you're bitter, aren't you? Bitter to the last.

Let me tell you something. Before I ever left an eye on you, I meant to end up in the old country. I don't remember the old tongue, though I heard it spoken on our own hearthstone by the old people — I didn't know what they were saying to be sure, but it was as natural to hear them at it as it was to hear the jackdaws above in the chimneys. I remember there was one saying that was always put at the end of the rosary by the fire at night. *Bás in Eireann* — Death in Ireland to you — that was my mother's wish for us all, that we'd make enough to end up in the old country.'

'There's only one way of making that wish come true,' said Mama, bitterly, 'and I can't see you ever having means for anything at the rate you're going.'

'You're wrong there. Like you're often wrong! And property doesn't cost as much back home as it does here, you know. A fellow was telling me the other day there are farms going for nothing — they're giving them away — in Leitrim and Roscommon.'

'Is it down there!' cried Mama. 'Thank you for nothing.'

Pappa sprang up from the bed.

'There you go again. What use is it trying to plan anything with a woman like you. God Himself wouldn't please you! It's my belief that you'll be disappointed in Heaven when you get there!'

'I wouldn't be surprised if I was!' cried Mama, 'I'm so used to disappointments now. But I don't believe you know what you're talking about! Leitrim! Roscommon! I'd never have a soul to speak to from day-up to day-down!'

'Like here!' shouted Pappa. 'How is it I have friends everywhere I go?'

But at this the tears started into Mama's eyes.

'Don't ask *me* that question, Dinny,' she said. 'Isn't it in the answer to it that all the trouble lies, that is between us now, or at any time? Oh, I'm so tired, tired, tired.' She raised her head and seemed to listen distastefully to the voices and laughter that came up the stairs from the parlour. 'You'd better go down to them; they'll think something is wrong. Or are they going to stay all night?'

'Oh God, no!' said Pappa, and he brought up another bit of Gaelic for the occasion. 'I'll give them a hint, one more round and call it a *deoch an doruis* — a drop for the door!'

'Aren't we really coming back, Mama?' said Maudie, when he was gone down.

'Why do you ask that?' said Mama, sharply. 'Wouldn't you like to stay in Ireland with all your uncles and aunts, and go to a nice convent school where the nuns could put a polish on you?'

It was four o'clock in the morning, and, if there were any daylight to see it, the coast of Ireland could have been seen, like a thin string of seaweed drifting on the horizon. As it was, all that could be seen was the flash of the lighthouse.

'Wake up, Maudie, wake up, for your first glimpse of Ireland. Look!'

Through the porthole, misted over now with their breath, all Maudie could see at first was the same grey waste of waters that had washed outside it every day of the voyage, except that now it was lit with flashes from the lights in the engine rooms. When her eyes became accustomed to the dimness, she could see that far out it was lit too by white flashes of its own cold foam. Then, suddenly, in the distance, a black fist opened to let out a blue ball of light, and closed again, then opened to catch it once more — closed and opened, closed and opened, closed and opened —

'It wasn't really Ireland? It was only old rocks,

wasn't that all?' she asked timidly later in the day, when they were in the tender at Cobh and still far away a green shore floated on the top of the water.

She was feeling very sleepy but she didn't fall asleep till they were in the train.

Then she sank back weakly against the red repp seats that smelled of dust and coal-fumes, and it really seemed as if she had only just closed her eyes when Mama was shaking her to wake and open them.

'Here, let me tidy you up,' she said. 'This is the next station but one to — there!'

Maudie knew she had nearly said "home", but had changed it quickly to "there". Tired as she was, she sensed an apathy in Mama. Where now was the impetuosity that woke her up to see Fastnet Rock?

And then — suddenly — before the train had properly pulled up on the platform — wrenching open the carriage door, shouting, laughing, kissing Mama, and seizing up their baggage — were three of the handsomest young men Maudie had ever seen. It was the uncles: the fabulous uncles.

'But we're only at the Clare Junction!' cried Mama.

'We couldn't wait!' cried the uncles all together, like schoolboys. 'We took a sidecar and came up here to meet you. How are you, how are you? Welcome home at last. Time you came back!'

Maudie was overwhelmed. Such laughing! Such kissing! No wonder Mama missed them so much, and was always talking about them, and telling about their larkings and goings-on.

'Is there anybody there for here?' cried Uncle Pauddy, as the train came to a stop again. 'Mind the step, mind the step,' he cautioned, as they got out on the palely lit station. 'Take my arm,' he cried, as they stepped into the pitch black street behind the station.

'I know my way,' said Mama, irritably. 'What about

the trunks?' But Uncle John-Joe was already loading the trunks on to a little trolley that was standing up against the wall.

'We use it for bringing the porter barrels out to the bottling shed,' he explained to Maudie. 'Did you ever hear of porter, I wonder?'

'Is it like lemonade?' she ventured. They all laughed.

'Poor Dinny!' said John-Joe.

'So you remember that after all the years!' said Mama.

'How is he, anyway?' said Matt, quickly.

'Oh, he's fine,' said Mama.

'I'm glad to hear it,' said Matt, soberly. 'He'll be over after you it's likely.'

'That's what he planned anyway,' said Mama, shortly.

'That'll be grand,' said Matt. 'We might persuade him to buy a little place over here and settle down in it for good.'

They were well out of the station now, in a narrow street with no footpath, walking abreast in the middle of the road that was soft and muddy.

'Don't tell me there was a Fair today,' said Mama, as she splashed into a puddle.

'Oh, indeed, yes,' said John-Joe, apologetically. 'Today was the second day of the big October Fair.'

'What a day I chose!' cried Mama.

'Come now,' said Matt. 'Don't start acting like a returned Yank.'

'That's what I am though, I suppose,' said Mama.

'Oh, not at all,' cried Matt. 'Sure you were only out there on a little holiday — you'll all be stopping home for good this time — wait and see.' He squeezed Maudie.

But Mama was going back reflectively on Matt's words.

'A holiday is it?' she said. 'Ten years! It was a long sort of holiday!' Then she laughed. 'According to Dinny, *this* is the holiday,' — 'Coming back is the

holiday according to him!' They walked on a few
steps more. 'I wonder which of you is right?' she said,
but as they went around a corner, she suddenly clapped
her hands. 'My old room!' she cried. 'All lighted up.
Oh, how good of Cass! How is she? How is Cass? To
think I never *asked* for her. Look, look Maudie,' she
pointed to a pink light that glowed away at the end
of the street. 'That was my room when I was a girl —
in the gable-end,' she cried. 'Oh, I've been so homesick
for that light: for that room.' She started to run. And
when they got to the hall-door she made straight for the
stairs, calling back over her shoulder, 'I forgot to tell you
that the dwelling-rooms are over the shop.' But Maudie
was staring about her enthralled.

All up the stairs, and all along the red-papered corridor at short intervals, fastened to the wall were red tin
lamps. Behind each lamp was a fluted tin reflector that
threw out a light so bright the red wallpaper seemed to
bleed.

At last she got to the end of the corridor and she saw
a small woman standing there.

'Cass!' cried Mama, and she ran forward.

'I didn't come down because——'

'Oh, why should you!' cried Mama, as they came
together and kissed.

'Well?' said Cass, stepping back. 'How are things?
How is Dinny?'

'Oh, he's grand — grand,' said Mama.

'I hope you weren't expecting to be in your own old
room,' said Cass then. 'I moved into it; I didn't think
you'd be back,' she added, defensively, 'unless on a holiday.'

'Oh, that's fine,' said Mama. 'Put us anywhere at
all. I'm so tired I'd sleep on the floor!' But she stopped
midway in the doorway of the room. 'What else is this
but a holiday?' she asked.

Cass said nothing.

'Did you think I wasn't going back to him?' asked Mama.

At that Uncle Matt came up with a trunk on his back.

'We're going to make Dinny buy a placc over here!' he said. 'And now, Cass, what about a cup of tea? And what will the child take? How about a bottle of lemonade? Eh?'

'Is it at this time of night?' cried Mama. 'Well, she'll have it in bed if so! I'll be undressing her while you're getting it,' and they went into their room.

'Will you be all right?' asked Cass, and she went out and closed the door.

When she was gone, Mama looked around the room.

'I must say I can't blame her for moving out of *this* room,' she said. 'I had no idea it was so ugly and dark. And over the shop! Listen!' From below there was a sound of feet echoing as if in an empty place. 'That's Pauddy getting your lemonade,' she said, and she frowned. 'Now, my *old* room was over the snuggery,' she said, as she pulled down the sheets. 'There was never a sound. I'm not complaining, of course. And, anyway, I know what's at the back of it all.' She lowered her voice. 'Jealousy! You see, I ought never to have had the best room, seeing I was the youngest daughter. But,' and here Mama whispered so low Maudie could hardly hear her, 'I was your grandma's favourite,' she said. 'She always spoiled me. Aunt Cass resented it. I didn't realize it till this minute. And, as I say, I don't blame her for taking it when I went away. Only I do think she could have let me have it for this visit.'

So it *was* only a visit. How the limits of their stay swelled and shrank, although thinking of the glowing ruby walls and the beautiful fluted reflectors at the back of the lamps, she felt that she would never want to leave such a palace. Why, the windows had alternating panes in diamond shape of red and green glass. Stained glass!

A palace indeed! And on the landing just outside their door she had seen a big pedestal, on which stood a brass urn filled with ferns. And the pedestal was marble. Truly a palace!

The next day Maudie woke before it was light. She was up and dressed in a minute and out on the landing.

Oh, but where now was the bleeding red wallpaper? Alas, unlit, the lamps shed no sanguinary glow, and the fluted edges of the tin reflectors were blunt with rust. As for the marble pedestal! When she laid her hand on it, it had the soft warm touch of wood! The red veining was done with paint. The marbling only a fake. And moving across the veined surface, were — that settled it — little putty-coloured creatures like the ones that crawled on the pews in church — that Mama told her were wood-lice. She stood and surveyed. Ah well, it was very clever of them to make it *look* like marble. But she was prepared for the stained-glass windows on the landing to be faked as well.

And true enough, they were only plain glass over which had been stuck transparent paper, patterned in diamond shapes of red and green. And where the paper didn't go all the way down to the sash, it was just plain glass, and you could see through it. Maudie bent down and put her eye close to it. It didn't even look out of doors, but down into the shop and there was Uncle Pauddy looking straight up at her, and next minute he came to the foot of the stairs to meet her. That was when he took her behind the counter and showed her how to manipulate the bottle-opener.

'Have another lemonade. Go on!' he urged recklessly. At eight o'clock in the morning!

It was funny how sick she got of lemonade in no time at all. Now, it would have been different with biscuits, but no one had told her to help herself to a biscuit any time she felt like it, although there was a big case of them in the middle of the shop with a glass lid on it. It was Aunt Cass who was in charge of the grocery though, and right from the start Aunt Cass had been critical of the free hand the uncles had given her.

'Aren't you afraid you'll be sick?' she said.

'I'm never sick!'

'Oh, that isn't what a little bird told me —'

The meanness of that! Just for spite, Maudie opened the lid of the biscuit tin and took not one, not two, but three big biscuits.

'You won't appreciate them if you eat too many of them,' said Cass. Then, looking out of the window, she gave an exclamation. 'Ah,' she cried, 'there's a poor child who'd give her two eyes for a biscuit this minute!'

Maudie swung around to see. At the shop window, looking inwards — but only for an instant — was a girl about her own size. But oh, she was so thin, and her skin so dark — or so dirty — and she had such ragged hair hanging about her shoulders! And only a glimpse was to be got of her — for as Maudie looked out, the girl, with a glowering look on her face, slunk off around the gable.

'Why don't you give her a biscuit?' cried Maudie on an impulse of malice to Aunt Cass. Then she had a better inspiration. 'I will,' she cried, and plunging her hand once more into the tin she brought up a whole fistful of biscuits and ran towards the door.

'Come back here,' cried Cass. 'Come back here at once. This is going altogether too far!'

But Maudie was gone. She rushed out into the dark street. At first she thought the girl had vanished into thin air, but as her eyes got used to the dark, she saw that she was still there, in a corner between the gable and the big yard-gate, and her bony shoulders were hunched

together the way angels are sometimes depicted in
holy pictures, their wings wrapped around them till the
white knobs of their wing-bones almost meet on their
chests.

'Hullo!' Maudie spoke exactly as if she was talking
to someone in no way peculiar or particular. 'Would
you like a biscuit?' she asked.

'I've no money,' said the girl gruffly.

'Oh, but I'm giving it to you!'

'Why?' said the girl.

'Well —' Maudie drawled to gain time — 'I got
them for nothing myself.' That ought to take the harm
out of them.

The girl looked more scared than ever.

'You'll have to tell it in confession if you stole them,'
she whispered. 'You'll have to tell the priest!'

And with a queer shudder, she was gone.

Maudie turned back into the shop. She saw uneasily
that Cass was talking about her. And Mama was there
too.

'Do you mean to say,' said Cass — very flushed in the
face — 'do you mean to say you don't see any difference
between taking them for herself and taking them to dis-
tribute in the street?'

'It shows the child has a charitable instinct, *I* think,'
said one of the uncles.

'That's not the way I'd describe the instinct,' said
Aunt Cass. 'But what is to be expected — the devil
makes work for idle hands — what is to be expected when
she's not where she ought to be — at school!'

'But Cass — my plans are so indefinite,' said Mama.
'And there's only the national school!'

'It was good enough for us, wasn't it?'

'Well, anyway, I'd have to ask Dinny about it,' said
Mama feebly. 'I don't know what he'd say. But tell
me,' she said more animatedly, 'where does that poor

child go to school, the child we were talking about just now, Mad Mary's child? I know she's to be pitied, but I just can't believe she can be normal, living in that hovel — and with that creature for a mother——'

'Is that the girl I saw at the gable?' cried Maudie, 'the girl——'

'Don't interrupt!' said Mama, fretfully. 'It has nothing to do with you. As I was saying,' she went on, turning back to the others, 'it's not that I haven't the greatest pity for the child. It's just that I can't believe a child like that can be fit company for——'

Uncle John-Joe interrupted.

'And what do you think should be done with a child like that? Where should she be sent, if not to the local school?'

'Well!' Mama hesitated. 'I don't know, but I'm sure that in America——'

'America! America!' cried Aunt Cass, angrily. 'If it was so wonderful why did you take her away from it? As for her making friends, I thought it was the company Dinny kept out there was one of your main objections to the place!'

Mama's eyes opened wide.

'Who told you that?' cried Mama.

'Who but you?' said Cass.

'Oh, Cass,' cried Mama then, 'you were always the same! A person might say one little word, only half meaning it, and you'd store it up for years in bitterness to throw it back in their face when they were least expecting it.'

'But you *did* say it!'

'Oh, what if I did!' cried Mama, and she turned to the uncles. 'She's put a different complexion on my words!' She looked around for Maudie and she threw her arms around her. 'Indeed,' she cried suddenly, 'it might be no harm to have the child away from the atmosphere in this house sometimes. Where's my hat? I'll go down to the convent right now!'

'Easy, easy!' said Uncle Pauddy.

But Maudie knew Mama. It wasn't only the lemonade that was coming to an end.

The school-house was at the far end of the town. As Maudie and Mama went up the street, beside them, running along in their bare feet with bulky satchels strapped to their backs, were a number of little boys.

'Are they going to my school?' Maudie asked.

'They have their shoes in their satchels, dear,' said Mama. 'They've come in from the country.' And suddenly she laughed. 'In my day they had to bring a sod of turf each for the teacher's fire. We brought a penny — the town's children I mean — I wonder if that old custom is dead? I must ask!'

Maudie was hanging back.

'Oh, Mama, look at those little cottages! Are they real?' There was a whole row of them — all dazzlingly white and all roofed with yellow thatch!

'Come on, dear,' said Mama. 'There's the convent. Look. Can you see it, out through that archway?' She pointed through an old stone archway that was right in front of them, and under which the road ran, as if it was nothing unusual at all for a road to run under the arch of an old abbey. As if it wasn't a road at all but a river! And as she and Mama went under it, Maudie shivered. It was cold and damp.

'Oh,' she exclaimed, for as she looked up at the glistening wet stones a big drop of icy cold water fell straight into her eye.

It was probably because of that she didn't see the cottage on the other side of the archway until they had nearly passed it, or it may have been that Mama pulled her closer to her side as they passed it, but anyway when she did look, she shivered again.

It was the same as the other cottages in a way, the same size, with a window to either side of the door — two eyes and a mouth — only this cottage had such sad eyes, and such a hungry mouth, and all around it was so dirty and dismal. There was grass growing out of the rotting thatch, as well as in the crevices of the tumbling walls, while around the door were pools of water. And in the pools there were green things growing — or was it moving? But Mama gave her a jerk.

'Don't stare like that,' she whispered. 'She'd think nothing of coming out and firing a stone at us, or emptying a basin of slop over us. She's done both before now to people, or that's what I've been told.'

So it was Mad Mary's! thought Maudie, but the next minute she felt so sad that the tears came into her eyes. Was this where that poor girl lived, the girl that had crouched at the gable? Was it here she lived in this awful, slimy cottage, in the shadow of the archway?

'What's behind the wall?' she asked, fearfully, because there were no more cottages now, only a wall of loose stones, entangled with ivy, and gappy in places, but never gappy or low enough to let be seen what lay beyond.

'Oh, it's only an old cemetery,' said Mama impatiently. 'There was a friary there long ago — that archway was part of it. But this is the school!'

For they were going up a neat cement pathway now to a school-house as neat as a shoe-box, with windows cut around all its sides. And when they got to it, and Mama pushed open the door, there were rows and rows and rows of scholars, and all of them staring outward, with open mouths.

'Ah, here's our little Yank,' said a tall young nun, coming forward and taking her hand. 'I don't suppose she knows any of the other children yet?'

'I'm afraid not,' said Mama.

But just then Maudie saw a familiar face.

'I know her!' she cried, and she pointed to where, in the very end form, and all by herself, the strange girl was sitting in a ragged black dress. 'Can I sit with her?' she asked eagerly, but she realized at once there was something wrong. The nun still held her hand. Tightly.

'Oh, but wouldn't you like to sit up in the front, Maudie?' she asked, and then, feeling Maudie pull back, she shot a look at the girl in black. 'I don't think Sadie Dawe would want you to sit beside her, anyway! I am sorry to have to say it, but Sadie isn't very friendly. That's why she sits down there alone. Sadie hasn't learned yet that we have to behave in a certain way if we want people to like us, and be friends with us.'

It was such a lie! Maudie felt sure of that.

'I don't mind *how* people behave,' she cried, 'if *I* like *them*! Perhaps she'll be friends with *me*.' And just like the drop of water from the arch fell straight into her own eye, she smiled straight into Sadie's eyes.

There was a moment of suspense. And then Sadie smiled back, right into Maudie's eyes.

'Well, you may sit there for today,' said the nun, giving Mama a conciliatory look, but Mama drew Maudie back for a last word.

'How can you be so like your father!' she whispered crossly. 'Why did you have to pick this child out of all the children in the town?'

'I'm sorry, Mama,' said Maudie, but she knew it was not for the present she made apology. It was for the future. Then she slipped into the bench beside Sadie.

The impulse that made Sadie smile, however, had died away. As Maudie gave a sidelong look at her, she saw that she had averted her face, and on it was a sullen, withdrawn look. Only once, when the nun was called to the door for a minute, Sadie turned her head.

'Which way did you come to school?' she asked.

Maudie looked her in the face.

'Past your house!' she said recklessly.

And after a minute that was like a shock of contact, Sadie not only smiled but gave a giggle. Emboldened by that laugh, Maudie whispered to her.

'What happens at play-time?' she whispered.

'They play!' said Sadie.

Maudie noted the pronoun.

'Don't you play?'

At last, Sadie turned fully around.

'They don't want me,' she said. 'It wasn't *true* what the nun said.'

'I knew!' said Maudie triumphantly. 'But I can be your friend, can't I?'

'Maybe nobody else will want you, now,' said Sadie darkly.

When the bell rang out for the break, though, a few minutes later, the other scholars all dashed out into the school-yard, and left them alone.

'I told you!' said Sadie.

They walked across the school-yard.

'What do you do?' asked Maudie.

'I sit on the wall.'

'Not all the time?'

'All the time. But you don't have to stay with me if you don't want to stay.'

'I do want,' said Maudie staunchly.

'Why?'

Why —? It was on the tip of Maudie's tongue to say it was because she was so sorry for her. She swallowed quickly.

'Because you're my friend!' she said.

And as Sadie climbed up on the wall, she climbed up as well. Sadie had her lunch in her pocket. It was in a greasy paper bag, and consisted of two slices of bread as thick as doorsteps, with a slab of butter in between as thick and hard as cheese. Maudie took out her orange.

'Is that all you've got?' asked Sadie, and Maudie was afraid she was going to offer to share the bread. But she didn't. 'The first day I came to school,' she said suddenly, 'the nun gave me an orange, and I bit it like an apple. I never had one before.'

Maudie was about to laugh until she saw Sadie's face.

'They all laughed at me,' Sadie said, 'even the nun.' She looked at Maudie.

'Do you know what I'd have done?' said Maudie — 'I'd have laughed too! I'd have *died* with laughing! And I'll tell you something! You'd have laughed too — if you saw someone else do it!'

But Sadie shook her head.

'I'd never laugh at anybody — ever, ever,' she said, '— no matter what they did!'

Maudie dangled her legs for a while after that.

'That's queer, you know,' she said. 'I bet you'll be different when you grow up.'

'No, I'll never be different from what I am now,' said Sadie passionately. 'I'll never be different from what I was that first day I came to school.'

'I'm sure I won't change much either,' said Maudie, but without conviction, and then she saw that Sadie wasn't listening. She was staring out across the convent garden that lay on the other side of the school-yard to where, because of the falling ground, the friary ruin could clearly be seen, and under its shadow her own cottage. At the door of the cottage there was a figure standing. 'Is it your mother?' asked Maudie, fearfully.

'Yes,' said Sadie, shortly, and then as the figure went in from the door, her shoulders slumped with relief. 'I always sit where I can see her,' she said, 'because if I saw her coming up here I'd— I'd—'

There seemed no words, though, to express what she

would do in a circumstance so to be dreaded. 'You see, she did come up once,' she said then, slowly. 'It was about me being told to bring a sod of turf. She said I was to bring a penny, like the town's children. It was all right, really, me bringing the sod of turf, you know. I didn't mind, because the arch is the boundary of the town and the country, and we're outside the arch, but my mother thought they were making other distinctions.'

'And were they? Was that what she minded?'

'Oh, I don't know,' said Sadie. She sounded tired all of a sudden. 'It wasn't that that mattered; it was the way my mother came in the door—' Suddenly she put her hands over her face—

'Was she—' Maudie almost said "mad." 'Was she very — angry?'

'No: no, she was very quiet and spoke very soft and polite, but what was awful was that everybody gave in to her, right away. We had a monitress, but she called the nun, and they both gave in and said it was all right for me to bring whatever she liked!'

'But wasn't that great?'

Sadie shook her head. 'It was awful,' she said. 'You see, they were *afraid* of her.'

It was out.

As she listened, Maudie felt so terribly sad she could only sit there dumbly, but after a minute she thought what a good thing it was Sadie knew what people thought. There would be no need to try and be tactful all the time.

'When did she get like that?' she asked casually, 'a bit queer, I mean,' she added.

'I think she was always not quite right,' said Sadie slowly, picking her words exactly, 'but she got worse after my brother died.'

'Oh, I didn't hear about that,' cried Maudie.

'Nobody talks about it,' said Sadie. 'It was because of something *she* did that he died.'

Maudie felt a terrible throb of fright in her throat, but the next minute she was reassured.

'Poor Ma,' said Sadie, 'it was her ignorance. And someone told her it would cure him; somebody bad it must have been: or someone worse or more astray in the head than herself!'

'What was it?' breathed Maudie.

'Well, he had a rash — only a rash, but someone told her to wash him in—' she paused, 'I couldn't tell you,' she said then, suddenly. 'Perhaps you can guess,' she added, her cheeks flaming. 'Anyway, there's the bell: we've got to go back to class.'

They didn't get another chance to talk till the bell rang at three o'clock. And then there was Mama, waiting for Maudie.

'See you tomorrow, Sadie,' Maudie called out. 'Keep my place for me!'

'I don't think there's any danger of your place being taken!' said Mama, coldly, 'and let me tell you, Maudie, that I'll take it as a favour if you don't talk too much about your new companion at the tea-table!'

But it was Mama herself, though, who talked about Sadie. Twice — twice at least — when Maudie came into the room she was talking about her to the uncles.

'— And wasn't there another child?' she was asking the first time. She stopped at once when Maudie came into the room. 'Never mind: tell me another time,' she said.

But the next time she went out of the room they were at it again. They didn't hear her come back.

'Oh, how revolting,' cried Mama. 'It's like something you'd hear done in a primitive tribe!'

'Well, poor creature, she paid for it — the sores became infected and he died — in terrible agony, the poor child.'

'Is it ever since that——?'

'I suppose so,' said Uncle Pauddy, 'although she was

never what you'd call all in it. For a while after the
marriage, and before the girl was born, she was normal
enough and she used to keep the place fairly clean —
she'd slap a bit of lime on the walls and one thing and
another, but after a while she lost heart, and — well,
that's how it started.'

Just then Mama saw Maudie. 'I thought you were
outside,' she said.

There was no more about the Dawes. Maudie didn't
know what Mad Mary had done that was so disgusting
and terrible, and she didn't really want to know.

'Were you very sad for your brother?' she asked next
day when they were sitting on the school wall.

'Well, nothing was so bad when I had him, if that's
what you mean,' said Sadie. 'We didn't ever talk about
things — like you and I do, I mean — because he was
too small. He was only seven. He didn't even have a
proper coffin, and that wasn't because we were poor
either. It was because he was small — it was only a little
white-painted box.' Suddenly she turned to Maudie.
'When they put it down in the ground and threw the
clay over it, I thought she'd go really mad, and I could
see people looking at her; they all must have thought
the same. I felt awful. Do you know what I wished — I
wished it was me in the white coffin. It being white, and
Tony being in it, didn't make it seem so bad to be dead.
It didn't seem as bad as standing there, with all the
people, and thinking she'd do something to make a final
show of me for good and all.'

'But she didn't?'

'No, she didn't,' said Sadie, wonderingly, as if that was
the first time she realized that this was so.

'I bet you were sorry for wishing you were dead too,'
said Maudie. 'Wouldn't it be awful for her if she didn't
have anybody at all?'

Sadie looked at her. 'I never thought of that,' she

said slowly. 'I am always thinking about what it's like
for me having her; I never thought of what it's like for
her having me. I never even thought — really hard
anyway — of what it was like for her not having Tony
any more.' Suddenly she seemed struck by something.
'Would you like to see Tony's grave? She keeps it lovely.
I will say that! And it's not easy to keep: it's not like
the new cemetery where there's no weeds let put up their
heads anywhere — the old friary is all weeds and briars.
You no sooner cut them back from your own plot than
they've rambled in again from the other plots.'

'He's not buried in the old friary, is he?' Maudie
couldn't help exclaiming. 'Isn't that very creepy, having
him buried just back of you?'

'I don't see what differ it makes him being there,'
said Sadie. 'And it makes it better for my mother. She
feels he's near her. And people can't be prying on her
and saying she spends too much time at the grave because
they can't see her going in or out — she gets over the wall.
There's a big gap at the back of the cottage, and Tony's
grave is only a bit in from that. There was a big patch
of nettles in the way, only she's flattened them down now
by going in and out, and the sting is gone out of them.
It's a lovely grave. She has lovely things on it, white
marble roses, and a little silver dove with a leaf in its
mouth —. They've come off other graves, but she didn't
steal them, you know, she just found them lying in the
grass, because nobody keeps up the graves there any
more, and the grass has spread out over everything like
a big cover: it has even grown up over the headstones in
some places: of course they were small stones to begin
with, I suppose, or broken. And some stones are sunk
down into the graves where the ground dropped. Did
you know a grave can sink? If the coffin is cheap and
caves in the grave sinks down in the middle. Oh, you'd
want to be careful there, I can tell you. You'd break

your leg or twist your ankle in a minute, and it's not lucky to fall in a graveyard — did you know that? If you fall in a grave you'll be dead within the year!'

'I don't believe it!' said Maudie, but all the same she felt a thrill of excitement. 'How do you know? Who told you?' she asked.

'Oh, I don't know who told me,' said Sadie, 'but you learn a lot in a place like the friary, just walking around, reading the tombstones. There's one man buried there with three wives buried along with him. What do you think of that? And the stone over them is split in two. I bet you don't know why?'

'It had to be moved so often, maybe, putting them all down?'

'No!' scoffed Sadie. 'The grave was robbed! Sometimes robbers used to dig up coffins of married women to get their gold wedding rings, and they thought they'd have a great haul with three wives in the one grave — but they got a land, because he used the one ring for them all : he didn't let it be put in the coffin with them — any of them — until he was dying himself and he had it put on his own little finger, but the thieves never thought of looking in his coffin.'

At this the bell rang. Sadie jumped down off the wall.

'Oh, I could tell you hundreds of stories,' she said.

'I didn't know a cemetery could be so interesting!' said Maudie.

'Oh, they're not all interesting!' said Sadie. 'The new cemetery is the dullest place you ever put a foot. I wouldn't be caught dead in it! though I spend a lot of time in the old friary. But of course I'm not like mother. I know that when you're dead, you're dead.'

'And doesn't she know that?' Maudie jumped down from the wall too.

'Wait till you see Tony's grave!' cried Sadie. 'I'll take you this afternoon.'

For the rest of the day, whenever she had thought of
going to the old cemetery, Maudie's heart filled with
pleasurable dread; but at four o'clock that afternoon
when they climbed up on the wall, and then dropped
down into the long yellow grass, she felt a different kind
of dread : not so pleasurable.

It was true the grass was never cut. It was tough and
matted. When they dropped down into it their feet were
immediately netted and snared, at least that was how
it felt to Maudie. Sadie took high springing steps and
never stumbled. Was it true what she had said about
falling in a cemetery?

'Oh, wait for me, Sadie,' she cried.

'Ssh, ssh,' said Sadie urgently. 'We don't want people
to know we're here.'

Maudie looked back over her shoulder. There didn't
seem much chance of anyone knowing. Always, when
she passed under the wall on the outside, she used to think
this place was silent and still. Now it seemed as if
it was the town outside that had gone silent, like a clock
that had stopped, while all around them sounds that
ought hardly to be heard surged into her ears. Their
own feet on the matted grass sounded noisily. The wind,
that only lightly stirred the ivy clambering over the headstones, yet caused the pointed leaves where they met the
stone to send out a mysterious tapping. And somewhere
in the grass to one side there was a strange sound, half
sighing, half singing, as the wind went over a rusted
tangle of wire.

'Oh, what is that?' she cried, drawing back. 'Is it
a rat-trap?'

Sadie laughed.

'It's an immortelle,' she said, but it was impossible for
her to make Maudie see what it had been before its glass
dome was violated and its false flowers broken and lost
in the weeds. 'Come on. I'm dying to show you our

grave. I can see it from here,' raising her arm and pointing.

But Maudie had hardly ventured to take one step after her when unaccountably Sadie drew back.

'Perhaps you don't really want to see it. Perhaps you'll get stung with nettles. Perhaps we'll go another day!'

'There's something you don't want me to see!' cried Maudie, accusingly. And, knowing now where the grave was from the way Sadie had pointed, she ran ahead of her, full tilt towards it.

The grave was like a little glade in the forest of dock and old nettles. It was a small rectangular shape, as neat as any grave in the new cemetery, and it was decorated, oh so beautifully, with all kinds of things, jam-pots filled with wallflowers, little plaster figures, and, as Sadie said, broken pieces of marble statuary, a scroll, a little white cross, and yes, firmly bedded in the loosened clay, a white angel with outspread wings, with only one of them a little bit — a very small bit — broken at the tip.

'Oh, but it's beautiful, Sadie,' she called back. 'It's just as you said. I don't see why you didn't want me to—'

Even as she said the words, though, she did see why Sadie had turned back. In the middle of the grave, among all the bits of mortuary marble and plaster, there was — or maybe she wasn't seeing right — Maudie went slowly forward — yes, it was a lemonade bottle : a full bottle, unopened.

Then Sadie came up to her.

'I didn't want you to see it,' she said slowly. Then she spoke terribly quickly. 'She doesn't do it very often ; it's a long time now since she did it at all. I thought she'd given it up, or forgotten, or something. I wouldn't have brought you only I thought that — but — now — well, now you've seen!'

A vaguely oppressive feeling came over Maudie, although when she looked around the graveyard, except for Tony's plot, it was only like a big untidy garden. Yet she felt the oppression growing, and she felt she was going to cry.

Sadie stared at her incredulously.

'I thought you'd laugh,' she said. 'I thought you'd be finished with me when you knew she was as queer as all that — I thought you'd say it wasn't any wonder she was called — well, what she's called!'

Maudie wiped her eyes.

'Well, I suppose you could laugh at it too, if you looked at it another way,' she said, and she actually tried to laugh — a bit. 'Does she think his ghost will come back and drink it?'

'I suppose so,' said Sadie, and they stood and stared at the lemonade. But, of course, it was a funny sight to see it sitting there on the grave. Maudie did feel that she might really laugh in a minute. She might have done so if only the sight of it had not reminded her of something else.

How odd it was that she had got so sick of the lemonade when the uncles were lavishing it on her at the start, and now, when they'd stopped forcing it on her, she'd got back all her wish for it! Wish for it? Why the sight of that bottle there on the grave was enough to make her throat as dry as blotting-paper. She closed her eyes and ran her tongue over her lips. She could just imagine the cap being prised up, slowly at first, and then jerking into the air, with millions of little beady bubbles welling upwards, and then pouring down the sides of the bottle. Not to lose one single bubble of it, she'd hold the bottle up over her head and let it roll down her throat. Oh, the longing that came over her! She opened her eyes. I'll have to go home, she thought. I'll have to humiliate myself. Even if it's only Aunt Cass that's in the shop, I'll have to humiliate myself and beg her for a bottle. I couldn't stand this.

But what about Sadie? Her glance fell again on the bottle stuck on the grave.

'I should think it would be to you she'd give it, and not waste it like this,' she said. She bent down and looked closer. The label was new and glossy. 'Is it the same bottle she puts every time?' she asked, but before Sadie could answer, in a clump of nettles to one side, under a bit of an old wall that once was part of the friary nave, she saw fragments of broken glass, one bit of bottle neck with the gilt cap still tightly clawed down upon its unopened top. 'Oh, what a waste! Sadie!' she cried suddenly, and she stooped down and picked up the bottle, 'wouldn't she be delighted — your Ma — if she came along and found it empty: if she thought he came back and drank it!

'Do you mean we ought to spill it out?' Sadie asked aghast.

Maudie was taken aback.

'Well, we *could* do that,' she said, 'but that would be a worse waste, wouldn't it?' Remembering something Sadie had said herself the first day they met, she lowered her own voice. 'Waste is a sin,' she said. 'Of course, it's all right for your Ma,' she said, glancing at the broken bottles in the nettles, 'she's not *responsible*, I suppose. But I don't think *we* ought to spill it away. Anyway,' she said recklessly, and not looking at Sadie at all, 'I'm thirsty. Are you? It's very hot here!'

For a minute there was silence.

'I'm *very* thirsty!' said Maudie again.

Then Sadie seemed to get limp, and she said something so low Maudie barely caught it.

'I'm gasping!' said Sadie.

'That settles it then!' said Maudie, and she grabbed the lemonade bottle tighter, and looked around impatiently. 'How will we open it, that's the thing?'

A reckless exhilaration was sweeping her onward. She
could see that Sadie was being swept along too. Her wild
eyes were no longer at such odds with her face. And a
rich red colour raced in her cheeks. And what was rarer,
she cracked a joke.

'She ought to have left a bottle-opener!'

At the thought of Mad Mary, Maudie swallowed a
gulp of air, but she was steadied by the thought that soon
she'd be swallowing the fizzing golden lemonade. And
after all, what they were doing was a kind of an act of
charity.

'Would we break the neck of the bottle, do you think?
We could hit it off a stone. Oh no — wait a minute.'

She darted over to the grave. There among the mis-
cellany of plaster emblems and bits of marble, was a strip
of metal with a Latin inscription. It might have been off
a coffin, she thought, but the thought only made her
giggle. She picked it up. 'This will do it!' she cried,
and wedging it between the little tight teeth on the rim
of the cap she pressed upwards with all her strength.
'Hurrah!' The cap flew up like a bird, and the foam
came slowly after it, swelling upwards first and then
falling down the sides of the bottle. 'Quick. Lick it,'
she cried, 'don't waste a drop!' She held up the bottle
in the air so that both of them, pressed together, could
catch with their eager open mouths the ineffable stream.

It was while they still held the bottle over their heads
that, under it, Maudie looked across the grave and saw
Mad Mary.

At the sight of that figure, silent and still, in her black
rags, and appearing like a spirit without any warning,
all the fears of her that had till then been dampened down
in her heart burst into flames of panic and terror. Not a
limb could she move; not a part of her, not even her
tongue, that had stopped in the middle of a lick. And
after a second Sadie, too, saw her mother.

'Oh Jesus, Mary and Joseph! she'll kill us,' she
cried out loud, as if the woman in front of them was deaf
to them. 'She'll murder us!'

Were they far from the gap in the wall? Maudie
wanted to turn and look, but to do so she would have to
take her eyes off the woman. And her eyes were all she
had to defend her. She stared into Mad Mary's eyes.
And then, to Sadie's amazement, instead of running
back, Maudie ran forward.

'We didn't mean any harm, you know,' she cried. 'It
was only going to waste!'

'I know that, child; I know it *now*,' said Mad Mary,
and she looked not at Maudie at all, but down at the
little decked-out grave. 'He's gone beyond where I can
do anything for him,' she said, 'and maybe it's as well.'
She raised her eyes and looked at Sadie. 'It'd be fitter
if I gave it to her. He was only a child, but sure that's
all she is too.' She paused. 'And what more am I at
times. Wasn't it only a child would have gone on like I
did, putting food on a grave? If I'd gone on much
longer like that I'd have been put away — and the right
thing for me.'

'Oh, that's no kind of talk!' cried Maudie.

Mad Mary looked at her.

'Whose child are you?' she asked, but she didn't listen
to the answer. 'What did you do with the lemonade?
Did you let it spill?' For the bottle had fallen from
Sadie's limp fingers. 'Would you like some more?' she
asked. 'Take her home to the cottage, Sadie,' she said,
'and I'll get some for the both of you.'

But enough was enough for one day.

'Let Sadie come back with me,' Maudie cried, 'and
we'll get some from my uncles. And we won't have to
pay for it,' she cried, appealing to Mrs. Dawe. 'Think
of all the money you've wasted,' she said persuasively,
and she nodded towards the nettles, where a bit of

bleached paper that had once been a glossy label now
fluttered dry as a leaf between the stalks.

'Your uncles won't want the like of her with you
maybe,' said Mad Mary dubiously.

'Why wouldn't they?' countered Maudie.

'That's right,' said Mad Mary. 'Why wouldn't they?'
and she looked at Sadie as if she'd seen her for the first
time. 'Do you never put a comb through your hair?'
she said crossly.

'I think we'd better go, Mrs. Dawe,' said Maudie
politely.

'Good-bye, Ma,' said Sadie.

'I'll be with you as far as the gap in the stones,' said
the woman. 'I'd be better employed doing a bit of
readying at home than always readying this place.'

'Oh, but the grave is lovely!' said Maudie. 'The
lemonade bottle spoiled it really. Didn't it?'

They all stood and looked back in agreement. Then
they went out through the gap in the wall and Maudie
and Sadie waved their hands at Sadie's mother and ran
through the archway back into the town.

But oh, what was that at the gable-end of the shop?

'A jaunting-car!' cried Maudie. 'A sidecar, I
mean!' On the top of it was a big corded trunk, that the
jarvey was just reaching up to take down. It was what
was on top of the trunk that took Maudie's eye. A
bowler hat!

'Pappa's!' she screamed. They were only two weeks
gone from him. Triumph, she thought, triumph. Here
he was following them. But she didn't know whose was
the triumph, their's or his. 'Oh, I must hurry!' she cried.

'I suppose I'd better go home,' said Sadie, sadly. And
then she caught Maudie by the sleeve. 'I suppose you'll
be going back to America now?' she said.

Maudie turned.

'Oh, I don't know,' she said. 'We might live here!

And what does it matter—' she stopped. 'We'll always be friends. And anyway, once you get started, friends are easy to make — you'll see! But come on quick. We're sure of the lemonade now that Pappa's here — lots of it!'

What's wrong with Aubretia?

THEY were standing inside the big gates at the entrance to the avenue: the gates that were one more anomaly now as the villas invaded the small fields to either side of the drive.

'Is there to be no end to them?' she cried, as if, because he lived down in one of them, Alan should know.

'I'm not the contractor. I've told you that before,' he said shortly.

'Yours was one of the first to be built though,' she said accusingly, as if this made him a party to the whole scheme. 'They levelled the little upland pasture last week, did you know that? And they're laying down a new road. Villas, villas, villas! They stick up like tombstones all around us. We might as well be living in a cemetery.'

'It can't be worse than when you first had to sell the land. I could understand your being pretty fed-up then.'

'Oh, it wasn't so bad then. We saw it coming, I suppose. And we really didn't realize there would be all this appalling vulgarity.'

'It was really the villas themselves you hated, wasn't it?' he said thoughtfully.

She pulled him up short, though.

'Why the past tense?'

He was a bit startled by the sharpness in her voice, but he answered off-handedly all the same.

'Well, you must be getting used to them by now, no matter what you say.'

'As if I ever could,' she said passionately.

Still, they did not quarrel then. He looked up at the

big granite pillars to either side of the gates, wound round with ivy, that having no more foothold on the stone, flowered and fruited wildly about the heads of the plaster figures (no noses) that held aloft the empty iron brackets of long-ago carriage lamps.

'The funny thing is, you know,' he said ruefully, and he nodded backwards in the direction of the new villas, 'to them it's this that is the eyesore!' He laid his hand on the granite pier, and nodded again, this time back at the dark old house in the trees.

'Is it an eyesore to you then?'

He paused for a minute before he answered her.

'Look here, Vera,' he said then sternly, 'I feel we are on to something more complicated than aesthetics. Are we?'

'Oh, not necessarily,' she said, but she also had begun to be uneasy as to where their words were leading them.

'I've felt it before now!' he said quietly. 'I felt it the day you were sneering at those people in the villa opposite us when they were planting the aubretia, do you remember?'

'Not sneering! I only asked why it always had to be aubretia!'

'You knew why! Because they didn't have generations behind them with experience of making terraces and shrubberies — like you!'

She agreed. 'Maybe so, but I don't see what it has to do with us now!'

'It has everything to do with us. I felt that day that it might easily have been *my* family that offended you with their horticultural ignorance — it could easily have been *me*. As a matter of fact I like aubretia. I don't see what's wrong with it.'

'Oh, for goodness sake,' she cried. She wished passionately that she could have retracted her own words at the start, but he went on doggedly.

'It's a question of class, I suppose?' he said.

'Oh, don't be silly,' she cried quickly, too quickly; the words were barely out of his mouth, and she had anticipated them too accurately. 'Don't be silly! Not class: taste if you like!'

But he wasn't convinced.

'Taste is the new euphemism for class.'

'Nonsense. There's no such thing as class nowadays; not in places like this anyway, not in any form.'

'You're right there,' he said. 'It hasn't any form any more. It's formless and vague, like a fog. You get lost in it. At least that's how I'd feel, I'm sure, if I was talking to your father. What does he think of me, by the way?' he asked suddenly. 'He must have noticed my calling for you so often.

It was so sudden a twist to the conversation that her heart missed a beat. With the simple question, they had soared suddenly above the reach of the small vexations that troubled them.

'I'll have to get to know him, sooner or later,' he said.

'Would you like to come to tea some afternoon', she asked cautiously, 'what about some Sunday afternoon — next Sunday?'

Oh that afternoon! How awful it was. Her father was at his worst.

To begin with, because Alan lived in one of the villas, her father acted as if they were in the relation of tenant and landlord. She was mortified, though she ought to have foreseen it. It was the way he went on all the time since the villas started. He acted as if, erected on his land, he had an interest in them. The way he walked around studying the layout of the foundations, criticizing the workmen, questioning the mix of the cement. Of course, he had gone on much the same way years before they ever sold the land, when they first had to let it for grazing. That ought to have been his first come-down,

but he never gave in to it. He walked around the pastures
as usual, with his stick that had a small hoe at the end,
scotching thistles, and prodding the dealer's cattle.

'It's time those pollies went to the sales yard,' he'd
say. 'They'll only lose weight in this weather.'

Ah well! it had done no harm to anyone then. But
now before Alan she could hardly bear it.

She could see, the minute he came into the room that
Alan was thunderstruck at the discrepancy between the
old man's squirish notions, and his most unsquirish
manners. His manners were at their worst that day.
When tea came in, he was the limit. He pounced on the
food, re-buttering the buttered bread, clapping two or
three slices together and stuffing them into his mouth like
a sword swallower. As for his cup, he took it straightaway
out of the saucer and set it on the floor between his legs.
The only use he made of the saucer was to slop the tea
back and forth from it to his cup to cool it. And once,
having made it too cold, he reached out and snatched
the lid of the silver kettle that swung on its silver tripod
over the lighted spirit lamp, and slopped back his whole
cupful of tea, regardless of having already drunk some of
it, regardless of its being poisoned with too much sugar
and cream.

Yet the really awful thing was that it was Alan, and
not he, who appeared in a bad light! It was Alan who
looked at a disadvantage. Take the way they each acted
if she had to stand up for anything, or even half-stand,
for any reason. Father, as usual, sat tight. But poor
Alan sprang to his feet tirelessly every time, even if she
only as much as stirred in her chair to reach for another
cup. He must have jumped up a dozen times in this way,
till at last it seemed to her that the gesture was drained
of courtesy, and had become like an uncontrollable dis-
ability — a tic!

'Oh, do sit down; you're like a jack-in-the-box!' she

said at last, and she knew she had hurt and perplexed him.

All the same, later that same day, when she was walking part of the way down the driveway with him, on his way home to the villas, she was not prepared for the effect the visit had had upon him. Their relationship seemed unaccountably to have deepened. At the gate he put up his hand to his forehead.

'What are we going to do?' he asked morosely.

'You're not proposing to me, by any chance, are you?' she said caustically, because she, too, was upset, and it was a joyless moment, anyway. It called for bitterness.

'No, I'm not,' he said quietly. But he smiled. 'I'm afraid I took it for granted, right at the start, that you'd have me, if circumstances were otherwise.'

At first his words filled her with such joy that she missed the ominous note at the end.

'— What I mean is this, Vera — we'd have to go away. We couldn't stay here! You can see that!'

'But why on earth . . . why can't . . . ?'

At thirty-four, she had for a long time become unconsciously reconciled to the thought that she would not marry, and in the unexpected, tumultuous happiness of being in love with Alan she hadn't given any thought to the practicalities.

Once or twice it had crossed her mind to wonder where they would live, but it had never seemed urgent. She had even looked around the old house sometimes, and thought how easy it would be to make separate quarters for Father if—

'But why?' she said again.

'Why what?' he said roughly.

'Why would we have to go away? What about your work? And there's father——'

'Oh, there's father all right!' he said sarcastically.

'What do you mean?' she asked, but her next words

showed her uneasiness. 'I think lately he looks very —'
she hesitated to say he looked old, however, although
Alan knew she was the child of a late marriage,— 'very
shaken,' she said. 'He needs me.'

'He needs someone. He couldn't stay alone in that
great barracks. But it doesn't have to be you. I want
you, Vera, but I'm not fool enough to think our marriage
would survive long if we stayed around here.' He waved
his hand to take in not only the old house and the masses
of oppressive ivy, but the entire building estate.

'Tell me one thing,' she said suddenly. 'What are we
running away from? This — or that?' and she nodded
first at the old house, and then at the villas and the
white cement roads that had been laid down, like the
runways of an aerodrome, and lit up in all their bareness
by bright arc lamps.

'Oh, don't try to be funny,' he said. 'It's the constant
comparison I can't stand. You think I hate the old
house — that I haven't the taste to appreciate it : it's
not that though.' He stared back at it. 'I feel it's brow-
beating me all the time : I feel I'm always being measured
up against it, and being found short !'

'Oh, for goodness' sake,' she said lamely. 'You told
me once that I had a bee in my bonnet about the new
villas : it's you that has one I think.'

'Perhaps it's the same bee,' he said drily. 'I didn't
honestly notice much difference between one house and
another until I met you. I used to hear my mother, and
the people next door to us talking about this old house,
and saying it ought to have been pulled down — that it
spoiled the whole estate.' He laughed suddenly. 'They
used to wonder if they could take an action against the
builders for leaving it standing to disfigure the landscape !'
She smiled wanly to please him, '— but outside of casual
conversations like that, as I say I was indifferent to all
houses ; a place to sleep and eat : that's all any house

was to me. I dare say I was lacking in perception of
some sort, but there you are!'

'Oh no, I wouldn't say that,' she cried. 'That *is* all a
house ought to be, I suppose, if——'

'Oh no,' he said then, grimly. 'You can't retract
like that, Vera. It was you who opened my eyes. Left
to myself, I would probably have thought the villas were
the last word. I'd have thought I was doing well by any
girl if I provided her with a nice new bungalow. After
all, it takes about twenty years of a man's life to pay for
one of them.' He was watching her face. 'You never
thought of it like that, I suppose? And I'm sure your
father never did! It must be a great thing to get to his
time of life without ever facing reality. No wonder he's
so fit!'

'Oh, do you think he's looking fit?' she cried, not
exactly irrelevantly, but with a relevance too deep for
him to see. 'I think sometimes lately——'

'Nonsense. I never saw a man of his years look as
active and strong. He could see us all down, that man.
I shouldn't be surprised if he outlasted the old house too,
in the end.'

They had turned at the gate and walked back, so that
now they were close to the house, and it loomed over
them, darkening the starry sky.

'I wonder what will become of it in the end,' he said,
almost casually, and she was suddenly chilled to the
heart's core by the impersonal note in his voice.

'Do you?' she said coldly. 'It will fall down, in the
long run, I dare say.' Then she felt a return of the un-
accountable venom the villas roused in her. 'Lovers will
make use of it, I suppose! They may complain about us,
but I often wonder what they'd do without our avenue —
and our shrubs!'

For there was always a couple, or more than one,
among the shrubs in the evenings. She and Alan could

sometimes hear muffled voices, or the creak of a twig to one or other side of them. They could even see, indistinctly, some of the less discreet pairs just inside the gate, pressed against each other in the darkness.

'Those are not girls from the new houses!' Alan protested sharply. 'They're servant girls.'

'I thought there were no servant girls needed in the new labour-saving houses?'

'Maybe not,' he said slowly. 'I don't know where they come from, but I resent your inferences.'

'You resent everything I say lately.'

But he didn't take it up. He was still thinking about the lovers.

'I suppose there were always lovers hanging about here, anyway,' he said. 'Someone was telling me that the road behind our house was once a lane, and it was known as Lovers' Lane. That's the way it's marked on an old ordnance map.'

'They had the ditches then, at least,' she said coldly. 'They didn't obtrude themselves on us. They didn't make use of our driveway.'

'You seem to think that a good thing,' he said drily. 'I'm sure they went a lot further with their love-making in the ditches.'

'Well!' she said defiantly. 'I'm sure it was more natural than this — this pushing against each other! And not so revolting!'

'Hhmmm!' said Alan. 'It seems morality also is synonymous with aesthetics!'

But he was less tense. And he even laughed. He probably knew as well as she did that obscurely she resented their own fastidiousness. Only for not wanting to put themselves in the same category as the unseen lovers in the darkness around them, there might have been more body in their own affair. But as it was, they always walked scrupulously apart when they reached the avenue, and at the top of the steps they kissed, by leaning forward towards each other, not moving closer. She, for her part, felt that he was holding back from her, and she felt, too, that it was for reasons other than a respect for her person. Obscurely she felt this too had something to do with the old house. If they had met in some other situation, in another city perhaps, would things have been quite the same?

'Well, Vera, what are we going to do?' he said again.

'We don't have to decide tonight, do we?' she said. 'I must go in. After all, there's no great hurry, is there?'

But he put out his hand.

'Vera, wait! I must tell you something else. I was all right until I met you. I mean I was satisfied with myself, more or less. But you've unsettled me. And whether you come with me or not, I'm going to make a change; to get away from here. As a matter of fact I didn't tell you, but the other day I saw an advertisement for a job abroad. I answered it. And I got a reply. I can take it if I want. What do you think?'

'It might be a solution,' she said cautiously, but even then she was sure he meant that he would go first and, afterwards perhaps, if she could arrange something for her father, or if perhaps — well, in the natural order of events poor father mightn't be so long in it — she'd be following him. She didn't dream for a moment that he intended to make a clean cut.

'But why?' she cried out, when she suddenly realized that he wanted things settled for once and for all. 'Why has everything come to a head so quickly? Why cannot we wait?'

'Wait for what? Till the old man dies? Till—?'

He stopped. But she knew, for all that, exactly what he had been going to say. He wanted her; she didn't doubt it, but he didn't blink the fact that she was four years older than him, and that each year they waited

would be a loss, not a gain, to her. He was so terribly
practical.

'I see,' she said.

She did see.

When they first met, he was always telling her how he
spotted her the first day she was out for a walk on one of
the new concrete roads. 'That's the kind of girl for me,'
he had said. It made her so happy to hear him say so,
but even at the time she noticed that he had not said she
was "the" girl for him, but only "the kind of girl" for
him. He had no time for what she called love, and absolutely none for love at first sight. Doggedly he claimed
that men and women selected each other consciously,
that it was a reasoned choice. The most he would concede to fate or fortuity was a slight biological attraction
between two people that they would have to examine
later.

With her it had been entirely different. It was his
unlikeness to her friends that she noticed first, but she
soon saw that they were only external disparities. And
when their eyes met even on that first occasion, she felt
that deep inside them was some affinity that when it was
brought to light ought to make him hers for ever. In
short, she believed in love. But apparently she was
wrong. It had been her undoing, that reliance upon a
fated bondage. He would not be hampered by any such
romantic notions. Indeed, he would not keep up a
vague association that could come between him and a
new attachment if he met another girl who was also his kind.

'Very well, Alan,' she said. 'If that's the way you
want it. But I'll see you again, I suppose — tomorrow?'

Did he hesitate? She couldn't really tell, but he was
emphatic enough in his reply.

'Good lord — yes! What do you take me for?'

But what did she take him for? And what was he —
to her, now?

A feeling of separateness, and aloneness that she had never known, even before she met him, a feeling of being sundered, came over her as she stood listening to his footsteps going down the drive. She had a sudden desperate longing to run after him, but it seemed that the shrubs were all eyes, hidden eyes, watching her. She felt sick too, and dizzy. She turned and went up the steps. On the top step she had to stand and draw a long breath, holding on to the big brass knob in the middle of the door, the big knob shaped like the head of a lion, and bright from handling except in the tangles of his mane where verdigris had lodged.

While she stood there the whistle of a train shrilled out and she started. Alan could not have got as far as the end of the avenue, and yet that whistle seemed to menace her; to sound his farewell. But he was not going away for several — weeks? Days? She hadn't asked him when he was going! The whistle shrilled again in the sharp night air. He might have been going tonight for all she knew. But no — he had agreed they would see each other again. She was nervy and upset, that was all. She'd see him again, and it wouldn't be a final meeting either. He wouldn't really go, or if he went he would write, and they would keep in touch. Yet in spite of all her efforts to reassure herself, her eyes filled with tears, and when at that moment the train whistle went for the third time, she steadied herself against the door. She really was dizzy: and in the darkness she saw the train rocketing through the night, all lit up like an excursion train, its golden lights strung loosely together and swaying gently with the sway of the carriages.

'I must be ill,' she thought in panic, because normally no train could be seen from the house. There was an old disused railway line somewhere near, on which a freight car was sometimes shunted to and fro. But no train. No brightly lighted train.

'I'm sick, or I'm going balmy,' she thought, and she dried her eyes and turned to stumble into the house.

As she turned, she saw the lights again, clearly this time, through the few remaining trees that stirred in a light wind, and made it seem that it was the lights that swayed. But the lights were not moving at all, for they were in fact the lights of the new villas, twinkling severally through the branches. Seeing what they were, her heart was assailed, for they struck an unexpected note, a sweet elegiac note that ought properly only to have come from beauty.

Bridal Sheets

I DECLARE to God, I'd liefer be inside washing the corpse with them, thought Peigin, as she caught the sound of tittering from the women in the room beyond the kitchen. She — God help her — had to sit all night in the kitchen with the new-made widow. Peigin gave her a baleful look. And she sighed. It was a sigh that drove out the sound of the sea that, else, was ever and always sounding in their ears, as it washed the four shores of the small island.

'Ah wisha, will you quit saying we none of us know what you're going through,' she said. 'Sure — isn't losing one's man a common class of a sorrow altogether in this island, or any other island of the western wave? Doesn't the sea get them one and all in time!' And she turned away from Brede in disgust at her moaning.

But after a minute she looked back at her in curiosity. 'I wonder would it be because you came here from the inlands, and not used to the way of the sea with a man, that you're taking on this way?' she asked.

For the man that was being readied for his wake in the other room had brought Brede with him, when he came back from the middle fields of Ireland along with the others on the island that weren't eejits enough to be taken in for ever by a government scheme, even though they'd been eejits enough to go at the start.

This scheme had a two-fold purpose: to assist the islanders and to spread the blas. Blas is a name for describing the true flavour or taste of the Gaelic language on the tongue of native speakers. The idea behind the scheme was to coax the native speakers up to the rich counties of

Meath and Kildare, and give them twenty or thirty-acre holdings of the fat pasture lands up there with a new cement house thrown in, and all for no more on their part than putting this blas of theirs on the tongues of their neighbours.

The trouble was that when the islanders got up to Bohernameen in the midlands, they found it wasn't only the blas that was lacking : the people up there didn't have one word at all of the Gaelic, and if they themselves weren't quick to pick up a few words of the English, their tongues might have gone idle in their heads. When, into the bargain, they found they were looked upon as oddities and land grabbers, and worse, they upped and made back for the island before the grass would grow over the stones again in their bits of fields, and the thatch fall down between the walls of their mud cabins. As far as they were concerned, the scheme was a dead loss altogether, unless maybe they might some day take it into their heads to drift over to Pennsylvania or Philadelphia, where they'd make use of the bit of English they'd learned. Indeed, those cities seemed nearer far than Bohernameen to them when they were safely back on the island, looking out from the shore of an evening, with only the waves of the Atlantic and nothing more between them and America.

Eamonn Og was the only one of the islanders who might be said to have got anything out of Bohernameen, and that was Brede. To listen to him boasting about her for the four short months he had with her, anyone would think she was the wonder of the world in the way of a wife.

Looking across at her again though, sitting lumpish by the fire, and moaning, Peigin began to think a man might pick a good wife away from the island, but he'd do well to look no further than the island when he was picking his widow he was! Such a hullabaloo! She was at it again.

'Ah quit it, Brede,' she said. What ailed her at all any more than any woman in a like case?

'Is it the sound of the sea ails you, Brede, seeing you're not used to it?' she asked suddenly.

Brede looked indignantly at her.

'You must think it takes little to ail me,' she said. 'Is it the sound of the sea? I put no heed on it no more than back home in Bohernameen, when we used to have plays in the Town Hall, and a fellow back of the stage would have a fistful of peas in a corset box and he rolling them up and down to let on it was the sound of the sea! Oh no, it's not the sea! Oh no, there's more than that ailing me, I can tell you, and none to know it. None to know it, I said it once and I'll say it again, and what is more you'll not stop me saying it, Peigin.'

'I'll not, I'm afraid,' said Peigin dejectedly, and she was silent for a few minutes, but she soon looked up again. 'I might think you had a bit of cause to carry on if there was a babby on the way, Brede, but sure that isn't the case with you — or could it be the case without you knowing, do you think?'

'It could not, thank God,' said Brede flatly.

Peigin crossed herself. Does God ever get used to being thanked for queer things, she thought.

Then another notion took hold of her.

Could it be the opposite of that altogether —? Ah but sure one had only to think of the fine man Eamonn Og was, to know at once he could handle any woman, and there'd be no holding back from him. And for that matter, mustn't it have been love that brought them together, seeing by the look of her Brede didn't have much on her back when she came to him. Her clothes were a holy show from the first day they laid eyes on her to this very minute, and as for the sheets that she'd given the women for laying him out, weren't they a holy show altogether, yellowed all over and mended in twenty places. They

looked like the very sheets that were put over and under
his poor father that died in a like way : sheets that were
in the house when she came to it, and in it many a long
day before that.

It would be a poor wake what with the sheets and
with poor Eamonn being a bit over-long in the sea before
he was picked up out of it.

'Are you worried he was so long in the water, Brede ?'
she asked timidly, meaning to tell her the island women
were a great hand at readying up a corpse in such a case.

But Brede turned up her nose.

'One hour in the sea or three days in it, what differ
does it make ?' she said. 'A man is a queer sight after it !
It's not like anything I ever saw. Back home in Bohernameen even if a man were to fall into a bog-hole, he'd come
out of it still looking like a man. Did I ever tell you,'
she said, brightening, 'about a man back home that
my grandfather used to know ? He fell into a bog-hole
one night after taking a few drinks, God help him ? Well,
he was never heard of more at the time. It was thought
he was gone off to America, because he had sold a heifer
that day and the price he got for it was the exact fare to
America in those times. And then one day about forty
years afterwards there was a body found in the same bog,
and who was it but the same man, and — here's the best
of it — looking like as if it was only that day he was after
falling into it. Preserved like a Pope of Rome, he was.
They only guessed it was him by the make of his clothes —
he had a swalley tail coat on him and frieze trousers — and
by a big turnip of a watch chained across his chest.'

'— and it still ticking, I suppose ?' said Peigin, who
had begun to have her doubts.

Brede gave her a look.

'It's the living truth I'm telling you, Peigin, and this
very man is above in the Museum in Dublin this minute
in a show-case for all to see.'

'For all to gawk at and all to gape at him? Glory be
to God, how can you call that a good thing to happen to
a man?' said Peigin. 'Well, it's true to say tastes differ!'
She stood up impatiently. 'I wonder if these women
inside would like a cup of tea?' she said, and she let down
the kettle two notches lower on the crane over the flames.
'I'll step to the door and ask them.'

It was the women had the questions for Peigin,
though.

'Is she still taking on the same way?' asked one. 'Ah
sure, God help her, it's my belief they know nothing at
all about death up there in the middle of Ireland. Do
you remember her telling us a story once about her own
grandfather that was sitting up by the fire with them
one night, and with the laughing and talking, it was a
couple of hours before anyone found out he was dead all
the time! Someone gave him a nudge to move over and
let them pull nearer the fire, and down he came on the
floor like a jug off the dresser! Now wasn't that the unnatural death! Think of that compared with the grand
death of an island man, standing up in his boat, maybe,
one minute, and those in the boats alongside him shouting
to him across the wind, and his womenfolk, maybe, looking at him too from afar off on the shore, and the next
minute he's gone from their sight, with one wash of a
wave, and his currach floating empty as a cockle-shell on
the sea. Sure that's what you might call death. Only
how could she see it our way being used to inland ways?
But, tell me, did you say the kettle was boiling? There's
a terrible drought on us, not but that I'd suffer along
another while sooner than listen to that one out there!
Oh, but look — is that the sun rising up?'

It was.

Between the two bits of sailcloth hanging over the
kitchen window there was a gap of brightness.

The woman ran over and pulled down the cloths.

'Glory be to God for the grand day that's going to be in it after all the storms. And maybe the seed herring will be in on the tide — oh look, they're in already. Look at them tangled in the weeds on the shore. The waves are swelling with them! Look! the pier is stuck all over with them, glinting like the sun itself! Oh, isn't it the great pity they have the grave to dig and can't be out with the tide!'

'Oh, but the grave is dug this hour back,' cried Peigin. 'I heard the feet on the shingle and I knew what was on foot but I didn't say anything,' she looked covertly at Brede, 'not but that they are the grand graves, the island graves.' Suddenly, with a warm impulse, she ran over and put her arm around Brede. 'They are grand graves altogether, Brede, not like the cold black clay they have over on the mainland, but fine white sand only, and it lifting on the wind in a way would put you in mind of the soul itself streaming back to its Maker. And if your eye should chance to fall on an odd bone, it's so rusted red with the salt of the sea air that you'd never think it was a common man at all was in it but a man of bronze or of gold itself!'

As she was speaking, an idea struck her and she sprang to her feet.

'Maybe you were never down there, Brede! How would you like to run down there now, this minute, and see the grave for yourself? Because I can tell you you'll not see it properly later with all the crowds that will be pushing and shoving to get near the edge when the coffin is going down in it! That's what we'll do! We'll run down there now in the first sparkle of morning. Where's your shawl, girl? Let you get it and come.'

'Where is my shawl, though?' said Brede dully.

It wasn't a very eager response but it was enough for Peigin. The next minute she had the shawl found, and thrown over Brede, and twisted around her, and had her out the door and facing down the boreen to the shore.

'It will give you a chance to have your cup of tea in peace and quiet,' she called back over her shoulder to the women.

'Glory be to God! Such a morning!' she cried, letting go of Brede, and coming to a sudden stop when they came in full sight of the sea, not hid now by any rocks or humps of land. There it stretched, blue, and still only for a few light ripples on it and a small breaking of spray around a solitary rock, far out from the shore. 'Come on, Brede,' she cried, and she started to run downward towards the sea-edge.

As they ran along the rutted boreen, one minute they'd lose sight of the sea and the next minute it would rise up again till it was like as if the island itself was a ship pitching and tossing in the blue.

And then, at last, they came to the graveyard that was marked off from the rest of the sandy shore by a ringed wall of big round stones, set unsteadily one on the other. Peigin hopped nimbly up and over them without knocking down one stone.

'Mind yourself,' she cried, as stones clathered down around Brede and she only after putting a hand on the wall. 'But don't you feel better now that we're here?' she asked, after they'd fixed up the gap again. And she straightened up and drew a big deep breath.

It was a grand thing after the long night to be out in the morning air. And, sure, if the sea brought death, it brought life too. The whole coast glittered with the seed herring. And it wasn't only the fish! She gave a little laugh unbeknownst to Brede, thinking of the big barrel of drink there was like to be at the wake that night, if some was still left from the barrels that were floated in on the tide from the French trawler went down beyond the Point.

'Aren't you feeling better now, Brede?' she asked again.

'Why would I feel better now any more than before?'
demanded Brede. 'Oh, it's easy seen you know little of
what I am feeling, Peigin!' she cried, 'or you wouldn't
ask that question,' and she lumped down on the wall,
knocking off a few stones again. 'Do you know what I
think? I think it's little you know about death at all in
these islands! And how could you? — the way it comes
leppin' at you, out of a wave, like an eejit creature that
would lep at you from behind a bush, putting the heart
across you with fright before you'd see what was in it at
all! Ah, but it's a different thing entirely up with us, the
way it can come gentle into a house, with no one seeing
it at all, maybe, for a while, and then one person maybe
will see it, and another and another. And the last one
may be the man it's come for — but by that time the house
is quiet and still and nobody giving him anything but
looks of pity and love, so that all can know their last looks
back from him will be looks of love, too. Not like this
place! Why here, maybe, it's in a fit of anger a man will
cleave down through the shingle, and he not looking
back even when he pushes out the currach into the little
waves and steps into it! And you left with that black
look for his last look at you!'

But Peigin could bear no more.

'Oh Brede, Brede,' she cried with a wail, thinking now
surely she knew what ailed her, '— was that the way it
was with you and Eamonn?'

But Brede turned in pained surprise.

'It was not,' she said sharply. 'And if that's what you
thought, let me tell you you're as far away as ever from
knowing!'

If Peigin's pity had flared up sudden, it died down
sudden too.

'Ach, I've heard that once too often,' she cried. 'If
you want anyone to know what ails you, then why can't
you tell it!'

'Oh, it's easy to say that,' said Brede, 'but would I be believed if I did tell it : that's the thing ! That's what I want to know. Would you believe me, Peigin ? Would you even as much as remember the big trunks I had, and I coming here, and they part of my story ? It wouldn't surprise me this minute if you'd forgotten all about them, in spite of it being only four months ago, and in spite of Eamonn having to get the lend of another ass as well as our own to carry them from the pier for fear our own ass would be kilt with the weight of them. Maybe the lot of you women have forgotten that entirely ?'

'Oh, but I do remember it, Brede,' cried Peigin. 'And why wouldn't I ? Wasn't it our ass that you got that night ? Oh, I was always wondering what was in them trunks, Brede !'

'What do you think would be in them ?' asked Brede.

'Ah sure, how would I know,' said Peigin.

At this Brede gave a big sob.

'That's true for you. How would you know ! How would anyone know ! All the finery and style, all the dresses and all the caps, and all the gloves and all the scarves and all the buckled belts and all the bits of ribbons for my hair that were in those trunks, so it was no wonder they nearly broke the back of our ass. How would any-one know it and not one soul on this island ever to see a stitch of them on me. Oh, isn't it me that is steeped in sorrow !'

Peigin stared at her. For the four months Brede was on the island no one had ever seen her in anything but the one old brown skirt and the one old black jumper that she was wearing at that minute. Indeed, it was one of the reasons that it was thought Eamonn must have married for love surely, when his bride had nothing more to put on her back than what was seen on her day by day.

'And why did you never wear them, Brede ?' she cried wonderingly.

'Ah, you may well ask! Isn't that what I'm asking myself ever since the first minute he was brought in to me dripping wet on the boards. To think he never saw anything but these old rags.' And she began to sob loudly.

Peigin could think of nothing to say for a minute.

'Ah whisht, Brede,' she said then. 'Sure you're forgetting your wedding day? Didn't he see you that day?'

Brede looked coldly at her.

'I can see you're not in mind of the day that was in it when we were married; the wettest day ever came out of the sky. And do you know the time we were married? At seven o'clock in the morning. Didn't we have the long journey back here to make that same day, and on top of that Eamonn was telling me about crossing the bay and how it would be maybe, with the boat rocking and rolling, and if my stomach wasn't right, how it's sick I'd be all the way over, leaning across the deck?' She paused. 'Well?' she said, 'were you never on that boat?' Did you never see poor creatures and their stomachs turned inside out, and it no use their leaning over the deck either, with the wind blowing back against them, destroying the whole front of them!'

She paused.

'Well?' she demanded. 'How would you like to be wearing your best blue coat and skirt in a like case? And it a light blue too that would show up stains something awful!'

'I wouldn't like it at all, Brede,' said Peigin emphatically. 'And was it destroyed they were on you?'

'It was not,' said Brede. 'Do you think I'd be that foolish as to have them on me?'

'Oh, but you brought them with you, didn't you?' cried Peigin suddenly. 'You didn't leave them behind you in Bohernameen?'

'Of course I brought them with me! But suppose you

had a fine blue coat for your wedding and you didn't
get to wear it on the day, wouldn't you be only belittling
it to wear it on a common ordinary day?'

Peigin considered this.

'How about Mass of a Sunday?' she said.

'At home maybe,' said Brede. 'But after one look
around the chapel here on a Sunday and seeing all the
shawls, I made up my mind that it would be out of place
to be dressed up in a new outfit that had the pleats still
tightened down with the tailor's tacking — I know the
way it would be taken — that I was putting myself up to
be better than my neighbours. And you know it too,
Peigin Mac. Don't you wear a shawl to Mass yourself!
You'd probably be the first to point your finger at me and
my finery. Aye, and at my hat too, with the grand brass
pin through the brim!'

'Oh Brede! And had you a hat too! Not blue like
the dress!'

'And why not? I like things to be a good match, although, to tell you the truth, the hat was a shade lighter
than the coat, but then it went with my gloves and my bag.'

'Your bag and your gloves? Oh, you must have looked
gorgeous, Brede!'

'When?' snapped Brede. 'Amn't I after telling you
the kind of day it was! — and it black night still when I
was going down to the church! And then the long train
to Galway — four hours I'd have been sitting on those
pleats — and after that the dirty old boat to get out here
— and you know yourself what came after that — the
cottage full to the door with all of you waiting for us and
the men stotious drunk by the time we got here without
waiting for the proper drinking to begin at all. Oh, that
night — I was jaded sure — if I had the dress on me then,
I would have slipped into the room and changed out of
it, in order not to have it rendered a rag in no time with
sweat alone! And anyway, that was one thing Eamonn

forgot to tell me, that there'd only be oil lamps here. Sure, whatever call a woman might have for her finery outside the door, she'd have no call for it at all inside with the smoke and the dark. Wasn't that the first land I got! And I knew well that it wasn't only that one night but it would be the same all nights, and maybe it would be that I'd never get a chance to wear one stitch of all that was in my trunk. And——'

'You didn't have *more* things, Brede?' interrupted Peigin, in amazement.

'Well, you don't think I brought the trunk half-empty, do you? Do you remember the size of it! More things! Hadn't I three pairs of shoes alone, leaving out of the count the black patent leather ones I was planning to wear at the wedding! Instead of that, the first thing I did the day after I got here was go down to the shop and buy these—' and she stuck out her feet with the coarse pair of men's boots that were all anyone had ever seen on her. 'One look at what you call roads hereabouts and I knew that was the end of my wearing my fine shoes! I never took them out of the trunk!'

'Ach, Brede. I don't believe you. I bet you were always putting them on at night for Eamonn, and the two of you talking about what it would be like if you were living in the midlands, where you could show them off to all! Oh, if it was Lorcan I swear he'd be out with a pick trying to level the boreen, and lighting fires on the big stones of a frosty night and throwing water on them in the morning to crack them so he could dig them out of it, and make it fit for me to be mincing down it alongside of him of a Sunday and he showing me off to all! Oh, men are divils for style, though they don't like to let on to it. What did he think at all of you not being able to wear them?'

But at this question Brede sobbed some more.

'Didn't I know I was right in saying you knew nothing

at all of what I was suffering!' she cried. 'Sure he never saw them, Peigin. Isn't that what's eating my heart out, how I was always thinking that I'd get a chance to wear them — that we'd go over to the mainland maybe or take an excursion train up to Dublin perhaps — and I'd give him a surprise when I'd take them out — but you know what happened!'

'Do you mean to say he never saw them at all?' cried Peigin, and then she threw her arms around Brede. 'Oh, God help you, sure you're right that I didn't understand. You're right about that: I can see it now. We didn't understand. Oh, God help you, you poor creature.'

Silence fell between them for a time, but after a bit Peigin began to try to seek out some little way of consoling the other.

'Come now, Brede,' she said half-heartedly. 'Don't take on so. Sure you're making it out worse than it was, I'm sure. Think back now. Weren't there little bits of ribbons for your hair or—' But suddenly her face lit up. 'Ach sure there must have been lots of things he saw if you come to think of it — and things no one else saw but him too — I'm sure you had gorgeous shifts when you had so much room for carrying them here in that big trunk. If it comes to that, what does a man care about hats and shoes! I don't believe they could tell, five minutes after, what it was we had on and we standing beside them at the altar! And why would they? It's not for them a woman is dressed on that day of all days, but for show! It's different altogether when they're alone together at last, the two of them. You know what I mean? It's only then they begin to see a woman.' A flush came into her face and she lowered her voice. 'Ah, sure God help them — you'd feel sorry for them really, wouldn't you: they get such a thrill out of seeing a bit of a shift, or a thing you'd wear inside next your skin. You'd have to laugh at them if you didn't feel so sorry for them — but God help them, you can't

blame them — from the time they're out of petticoats
themselves, people are always telling them not to look
here and not to look there and to keep their hands off this,
and their hands off that and slamming doors in their
faces and telling them to look another way! Even when
they start courting it's not much better, with girls going
behind trees and haycocks if they only want to straighten
the seams in their stockings. Sure it's a great excitement
for them the first night they can look all they like at a
woman, shift or no shift — you know what I mean, don't
you?'

But Brede was silent.

'You know what I mean, don't you?' cried Peigin
urgently. 'Not like us. Sure there's no mystery about
men for us. I was washing my father's underpants since
I was able to stand over a basin of water, and sewing
buttons on them ever since I could thread a needle. But
it's different for them — sure you know it is, Brede, so
can't you console yourself that way. Come now, let you
forget about the blue dress, and the coat, and even the
shoes and the buckles. It wasn't those things that Eamonn
was wanting to see when you were alone together at last.'

But Brede was still silent. At last she turned around
with a face of anger.

'Didn't I tell you I was jaded tired that night?' she
cried. 'Didn't I tell you my eyes weren't used to the
lamps? It was as dark as dawn in that cottage. Who'd
think of getting into anything good in that smoky little
hole of a room!' Peigin gasped.

'You mean you didn't wear your good shifts either —
ever?' cried Peigin.

Defiantly Brede set her lips, but the next minute she
broke down again.

'How was I to know that I'd never get a chance to
wear them for him at all?' she cried.

The two women sat silent for a time.

'Oh, what will I say when my mother hears I never put on a single stitch of the clothes she went to such lengths to have right for me, getting them taken up and let down, and let down and taken up till I was sick of the sight of them you might say.'

'Ach, bother your mother!' said Peigin. 'It's Eamonn not seeing them I'd mind.'

'Him too, of course,' said Brede, 'but my mother is to be considered as well. Wasn't it she paid for them? And the things in the other trunk as well. It was never unpacked either.'

'What other things had you, Brede?' cried Peigin, with fresh excitement.

'Ach, what do you think?' cried Brede impatiently. 'What do you think a bride would have in her other trunk but her bridal sheets. What else would you expect?'

But Peigin could only stare. 'And what in the name of God are bridal sheets?' she asked at last.

'Well, Peigin Mac, if it was back in Bohernameen I was and heard you ask that question, I'd be staring at you for a week! But seeing that I've lived here now for four dark months I can easily see that it would be a waste of time entirely for a bride in these parts to be having anything fancy in the way of finery either for herself or for her marriage bed, with nothing but dirty old oil lamps only good for filling the room with smuts! I don't wonder at you knowing only sheets made out of flour bags split up and sewn together, and hardly hemmed at all and the name of the mills not bleached off them! But oh, it's cruel to think of the dreams I had of taking the sight out of Eamonn's eyes with the sheets I had made for our wedding bed. Those sheets were the talk of the parish back in Bohernameen when I'd finished embroidering them and put the last of the lace medallions in them and cut the cloth from the back of them so the lace would show up, and washed them and ironed them! Everyone in the parish had to see them before I put them into that trunk. And to think that they never came out of it! Oh! oh! oh!' she sobbed, big awkward gulps of sobs. 'And to think that you'd claim to know what I was suffering! Not one woman on all this island in the memory of man ever had the like happen to her!'

'Oh Brede!' cried Peigin. 'How did you put up with us at all?' She threw her arms around her. 'Oh, God have pity on you,' she cried. And when over Brede's shoulder she caught sight just then of the currachs strung out on the line of the sky, and looking as safe as if they were only painted in a picture, she felt indeed that the sorrow which always and ever menaced her was indeed a bearable sorrow, and not to be compared in any way with the queer sorrow of Brede. 'God help you, Brede,' she cried, 'sure we didn't understand. Oh, aren't you the unfortunate woman entirely! Did you say he never set eyes on any of the style at all? — not even the sheets?'

It was a terrible sorrow indeed, she thought, and how could it be borne?

Suddenly she gave a cry.

'Oh Brede, I have it! Sure nothing is so bad it can't be worse. Why in the name of God didn't you tell me this sooner — and how long are we down here at all?' She threw a wild glance up at the cottage. 'Are they finished the tea, do you think? Have they gone back to laying him out yet, do you suppose?' — She turned wildly back towards the cottage. 'Look! There's a fresh bit of smoke coming up the chimney — they're after giving the sods a poke; it must be that they're boiling up the kettle again to put water in the pot. They say there's a great drought got out of working on a corpse. Oh God be praised, come on quick — isn't it good you told me! There's still time! You've a grand chance entirely to make up for everything. We'll get out them sheets and have him laid out in them. Isn't it a wonder you didn't

think of it! Talk of his wedding night! Won't poor
Eamonn be the proud man looking down from Heaven
this night and seeing himself lying in such grandeur! And
God knows he'll be fitter and abler to see them I'd say,
looking down from above, than he'd have been on the
night of his wedding, for sure he had other things on his
mind to distract him on that night. Oh come on, Brede!
'Hurry, will you! I can't understand how you didn't
think of it yourself! Do you remember that time
they were saying the sheets you gave them were a bit
yellow — a bit yellow! Glory be to God I didn't like to
say it then, not knowing you had any better, but they
were as yellow as the bill of a gander. Oh, isn't it
great that you don't have to disgrace the poor corpse
after all. Come on, quick!' and she lepped along another
step, but still not seeing Brede was hanging back.

'Peigin, hold your whist a minute,' said Brede at last.
'Isn't linen a terrible cold cloth to be laying him in? Did
you think of that?'

Peigin stopped, and then she gave a laugh.

'Will you ever learn, Brede! This is one night in the
creature's life that he's not going to heed the cold, God
rest him. Come on.' And she started off once more.

But they'd only gone a short way when Brede stopped
again.

'Peigin, I was thinking of something else. Linen is
terrible easy creased. Did you know that? I declare if
it wasn't for the medallions and the fancy stitches I'd
say that common sheets would look better on him in the
long run!'

Peigin stopped.

'Well, to tell you the truth, Brede, like you said yourself a while back, I can't say I ever saw any sheets but
ones made out of flour bags. What's the differ, anyway?'

'Ah, there's a great differ, Peig,' said Brede. 'Come
here,' she cried, and she went over to the stone wall to

one side. 'Linen is a very soft class of cloth. Take the
test for linen — you know that, I suppose?'

'I don't then,' said Peigin humbly.

'You don't? Well, come over here. It's easy learnt.
Say this stone is made of linen, and say this stone here is
made of an old flour bag. Well now, if you were to wet
your finger — like this — and put a spot of spit on this
stone here — the linen one — and if you were to do the
same then with that one — the one that's not linen —
why you'd know the differ at once because the spit would
soak into the linen one at once, but it wouldn't hardly
soak into the other one at all. Watch me, and I'll show
you,' she cried, and spitting on her finger, again she
dabbed one stone first, then spit again and dabbed the
other stone. 'Oh, but I forgot, they're only stones,' she
cried impatiently, as the spits stayed winking and bubbling
on the two stones alike. 'Well, I'm only trying to show
you that linen's a queer stuff altogether. I often wondered
how it is there's so much thought of it. It may be all right
for tablecloths, but I think it's a poor stuff for sheets, at
any time. I think maybe we ought to leave things as
they are, Peigin, for after a few hours those sheets would
be a proper show, all creased and crumpled!'

'Do you say?' said Peigin, and it was clear she was
terribly dejected for the minute, but the next minute she
gave a laugh and a sort of skip of joy. 'Ah, but we're
forgetting — sure it isn't as if the poor creature in the
bed will be twisting and turning — sure he'll have no
carry-on that would put creases in sheets. Ah, Brede,
you'll never learn anything about corpses, that's my belief. You're only looking for trouble where there's none
at all. Come on, and let you hurry too, for if we're late
and he's laid out already, you'll have cause then to be
sobbing and moaning, having lost your one chance of
making up to him for everything—' And this time she
caught Brede by the sleeve and gave her a pull.

But Brede pulled back.

'Tell me one thing,' she said. 'Do they bury the sheets along with the corpse?'

'Is it good sheets? Are you cracked or what?' cried Peigin, shocked. 'Why would they do that? What about all the corpses to come after? It's not every house that can say it'll only have one corpse, or two at the most, like your house — that is to say if you stay on the island, which I don't suppose you will?' But without waiting for an answer, she pulled the other's sleeve again. 'Of course they're not buried along with him,' she said, and then she stopped dead, as a new aspect struck her — 'unless you'd want it that way,' she said. 'But we can decide that later — that is if we are in time at all.'

They were in time.

'Oh, thanks be to God,' cried Peigin, when they went in the door and she saw the women only after standing up, and still wiping their mouths after the tea. She turned back to Brede. 'Tell us quick where you keep them, Brede!' she cried. 'She has grand sheets for laying him out,' she told the women, 'her bridal sheets. I'm dying to see them. Not that I think I'll wait to see them now, because if you don't mind, any of you, I'll run back to my own house and see that the fire isn't gone out. I might make a small cake of bread too while I'm at it because there isn't a bit in the house.' She turned to Brede. 'But I'll be back early before the crowds start coming so I'll see them medallions, Brede!'

'Oh, that's right, Peigin,' said the women. 'Let you go quick, though, because maybe you'd be able to get back in time to let us slip home for a while as well.'

'Oh, the lot of you can all go if you like,' Brede cried — 'it's all the same to me. You needn't think I'll mind being alone. Isn't it the last time I'll ever be with him! Wouldn't it be only right to leave us together for a while?'

The women stared at each other. Was this another

custom they had up in the midlands? 'What do you think, Peigin?' they asked.

'Ah sure, there's no knowing,' said Peigin. She went to the door. 'You may as well humour her,' she whispered. 'When you've all done, couldn't you slip away one by one, and maybe the last of you could slip away, a bit before I got back, if she insisted. You'd nearly see me coming round the Point from the door here, and that could be the sign for you, and it wouldn't be leaving her alone at all really, but only letting on to it.'

'That's a good idea, Peigin,' said one of the women. 'Let you go now and hurry back. And we'll get him into the fine sheets. Where are they, Brede?'

It was a bit longer than Peigin thought, however, till she got back and when she rounded the hill she saw the last of the women standing at the door of Brede's house straining her eyes outward. Peigin beckoned her to start, and she herself began to run down the hill.

'I was kept a bit longer nor I reckoned,' she said.

'Ah, don't worry yourself,' said the older woman. 'As long as you're here now, it's no matter what kept you. We've everything done, the poor creature wrapped in the fine linen sheets. And God help her, I felt sorry for her. She must have meant what she said about wanting to be alone with him, because even before I saw you coming she wanted me to go, God help her, and in the end she nearly pushed me out of the room, and she went back in to him, and shut the door! And isn't it true what she said that it's the last time she'll ever have him to herself because the crowds of the world will be here any minute for the wake.'

'That's true,' said Peigin, out of breath. 'God help her,' she said fervently.

And indeed, those were the words that welled up in her heart again as she stepped into the cottage and ran across the kitchen to rap on the door of the corpse room.

'God help you, Brede,' she said. 'Can I come in to you, because I'm in dread of not getting a good look at the sheets before the whole island is on top of us? I know you'd like to be alone with him, but if I get one gawk of the lace medallions I can sit out here in the kitchen till the first of the mourners gets here.'

She pushed open the door.

'What in the name of God are you doing, Brede?' she screamed, for there was Eamonn, and he turned over on his face, and there was Brede and she working hard, pushing one of the yellow sheets under him. And there on the chair, all in a heap, creased and limp where she had dragged it from under him, was one of the bridal sheets with its big dollops of embroidery and its big round medallions of lace. 'What in the name of God are you doing, Brede?' she cried again. But she knew. And Brede was too busy anyway to turn round.

'Mind your own business, you!' Brede said, 'and go back to the kitchen. I don't want the whole island in on me before I'm ready!'

My Molly

WHAT I couldn't understand was why my Molly took it so badly. We were only six months in the town at the time.

Most people were upset, of course. Why not? There wasn't a day in the past forty years old Sam was not to be seen, sitting in the window of his shop turning the wheel of his old sewing-machine.

I used to think he was like a sticky-back of himself pasted on to the window, if you know what I mean? It wasn't that he didn't look real, with his red face, and his bright blue eyes — the exact colour of the veins in his cheeks — and his big fibry eyebrows: it was just that you couldn't imagine him doing anything else; eating, sleeping, anything, only sitting there!

It was a shock to hear he was gone one day. Yes: like that. Like a snap of your fingers! No, I don't mean dead. People die every day, likely ones and unlikely ones! No: gone, that was all! Took his hat, put it on his head, and lit out: no one knew where.

It wasn't good, to think of an old man like that — like Sam, I mean — wandering about somewhere, maybe out of his mind.

Still I couldn't see why my Molly took on so badly about him. Not that I understand her that well myself. All unexpected she is: my Molly.

She's not a bit what you'd think from looking at her. Most people think she's delicate, just because she's so small, I suppose. Well, you should see the work she does! Her being so pretty gives people a wrong opinion of her too. It was like that from the start. Flighty, that's what she looks. My own mother used that very word when I

first told her I was getting married. 'You'll hardly have
a family out of her,' said my father. That was the worst
guess of all. We have five of them already, and no signs
of stopping I'd say for many a day yet. The money is
the only thing that would stop that. And money never
troubles my Molly at all.

'Don't worry,' she's always saying. 'I never knew
anybody to starve yet in this country. Something will
turn up, you'll see!' She believed a lot in luck.

I always felt, though, that there was a tribute to Molly
in all the luck we had. Luck isn't something you get
hanging on a bush. Some people attract it. She had
tact, too, or so I was told. A funny kind of tact it seemed
to me. I used to think tact meant always doing the right
thing, but after living with Molly I began to think it was
more like doing the wrong thing maybe and no harm
come out of it, but only good. Do you know what I
mean?

They're hard to understand, people like Molly. Even
when you're married to one of them for ten years, there
are still times you can't make them out. Take Molly and
old Sam. If it was anyone else in the town but Molly,
who went on like that I'd say she was putting her sorrow
out just for show. But there's no show about my Molly,
outside of her looks, I mean. Her looks are showy, I
know, but that was God's doing, not hers. She's true
to the bone, Molly.

Yet, there she was that day with the tears running
down her face. The news that he was missing went
round the town early. Then at midday the radio gave
out an announcement about him. Anyone who had seen
a person answering to his description was to go to the
barracks and give in their information.

'Now look here, Molly,' I said. 'I've had enough.
Don't carry on like that. I don't suppose you ever spoke
to the poor fellow.'

Well! you should have seen the look she gave me!

'And I doing business with him every other day,' she said.

Business? With a saddler? My Molly?

'Oh, I beg your pardon, Molly,' I said. 'I didn't know you'd taken up hunting!'

That was a good joke, you know. You'd only to look at us to know our social standing. Not that I believe much in class, but in a small town in Ireland you may not make any distinction between yourself and those below you, but you have to allow for the people above you making distinctions between you and them.

'I suppose you think you're funny,' said Molly. 'It was to get him to mend the strap of the go-car I first went in to him.'

'You don't mean to tell me that you brought that battered old go-car in to be mended by a man like Sam?'

Saddlers aren't two a penny in Ireland any more, and I got red in the face at the thought of getting the like of Sam to mend an old strap.

If only you could see the go-car, you'd know my shame. It wheeled out every one of the children in turn, and it was second-hand in the first place. But Molly knows no limits when she's bent on the good of me or the family.

'He was so kind,' she said. And she began to cry again. 'He came out into the street and knelt down and undid the string' — I winced at that — 'and when the strap was sewn he came out and put it on for me. Oh, I can't tell you how kind he was to me. And he told me to come back to him. "Don't wait till you get let down, my dear," he said. "Step in any time you have a spare minute and I'll put a stitch in it that will hold it together a bit longer." Which I did! He always did it there and then for me, he never charged me anything. I forgot to tell you that. It wasn't that I appreciated so much as his manner. You'd think he'd have no use for the like of me

compared with his usual customers? It was the other
way round! "There's a lot of the horse in themselves," he
said as they'd stamp off with their saddles and bridles,
"the bad points, I mean." Wasn't that a queer thing for
him to say, and his trade depending on them? It showed
how he trusted me. He liked having me come in and out,
I think. It was a change for him. He liked talking to
me, I think. In a way, I wasn't surprised when I heard
he was gone! From things he said to me now and then,
I think he had a notion of doing what he did for a long
time past——'

'Molly!' Was there more worry to come? 'You're
not keeping anything from the police, are you? What
kind of things did he say?'

'Oh, only just one thing and another,' said Molly, in
her vaguest voice.

'Tell me one!' said I.

'Well, there was one day he was out in the street with
me, putting on the straps, and a flight of birds went across
the sky over our heads. I don't suppose we'd have
noticed them, only the baby chirped. Lying on their
backs, babies see all kinds of things we never look at —
birds and trees and the sky itself. We looked up at those
birds.'

' "Queer creatures, aren't they?" said Sam. "I often
think it must be very tiring to be always flying about like
that."

' "Isn't it a curious thing, now, that if one of those
little birds was to fall down here in the street, you'd have
a crowd around it in a minute — a crowd as big as a
football match. It'd be a nine days' wonder!" And here
he looked at me with his little wrinkled-up face, and I
knew he was saying something important — important to
him anyway — "That's not the wonder at all, though,"
he said. "The wonder is that they keep on flying!" '

'Well? Go on!' said I.

'That's all,' said Molly.

I didn't know whether to be annoyed or glad. There was no need to go to the police with that rigmarole anyway, but how did it show he was going to disappear? Only Molly could figure that out.

'I hope the poor old fellow is all right anyway!' I said. 'Perhaps he'll arrive back as suddenly as he went — like the last time.' I thought Molly mightn't have heard he did it once before. It was over twenty years ago.

Molly knew all about it though. That's why she was so upset. 'I think it's a shame the way people are letting that influence them,' she said. 'Just because they made fools of themselves last time is no reason to think the same thing is going to happen this time.'

Now, I could not help feeling there was something to be said for people being a bit cautious, 'specially the Gardai.[1] Sure anyone can make a mistake! And the Sergeant was on holidays at the time. It was just that there was something unlucky about the way things happened! The whole town was leaning over the bridge watching the drag-net, the Gardai yelling and making themselves officious — I believe the young fellow in charge forgot his dignity altogether and pulled up his trousers, forgetting they were government property, I suppose, and went into the river up to his middle. Another of them let his hat fall into the water. Away it floated, with all the kids in the town throwing stones after it. It was a great moment altogether, I believe, when it went over the weir, and there was a rousing cheer from every man, woman, and child on the bridge. Undignified though: that's what the Superintendent concluded.

To think that it was at the height of all this — I'd say myself it was likely at the very moment the hat was going over the weir, wouldn't you? — old Sam got off the bus in the Market Square, and the Square as empty as if it

[1] Police.

was up for auction! And when the fun was over below at the river and everyone came back up to the Square, there was his sticky-back pasted to the glass again, the same as ever. No wonder the Gardai were lepping.

'It'll be hard to get them to drag the river this time,' I said.

'There are some people claiming he was seen in Dublin, did you know that?' said Molly. 'Did you not hear about the car? The Sergeant gave it out today that on account of the rumours of him having been seen, there was going to be a car hired, and he was going to ask for volunteers to go to Dublin and comb it out well before any more time was lost.'

'Well, isn't that a great idea?'

'Do you think so?' said Molly. 'It's all depending on who goes in the car,' she said doubtfully. 'They'll have a grand free trip to Dublin, anyway, I had a notion of going myself.'

'But what hope would the like of you have of finding him?' I cried. 'A little bit of a thing like you isn't fit for traipsing the streets of Dublin. It wouldn't be fair to take up a seat that might be taken by someone able and fitter than you—'

She gave me a look.

'It's because I don't like to see good money go to loss that I'd go! Don't you know poor Sam is dead!' she said. 'And there's all that money going to loss on a hired car to Dublin. Dublin: a place I haven't been in these two years, me that loved it so much, and me that needs a bit of change badly, as Sam himself was only saying a few days ago. I didn't tell you, because I knew we couldn't afford it. This would be a great chance, wouldn't it. I think I will go!'

'Would you do any looking at all for him, Molly?' I asked. 'I mean any *real* looking for him.'

Well, if you saw the kind of look I got for that.

'Shame on you,' she said. 'That's all I can say: shame on you! To think that I'd go gallivanting off on a trip like that if I thought there was the smallest chance of his ever being found. As you said yourself, I'd be a poor hand at sifting and sieving through the streets of Dublin. If I thought there was the smallest chance of him being found, it's you I'd make go in the car; not me. I do hope it will be fine,' she cried, and she ran over to the window and looked up at the sky. 'There's so much I want to get done. I'll get new vests for the boys — there's hardly a stitch left in their old ones — and I'll get some nice ribbon for the girls — you can't get the real good stuff in a country town, and it doesn't cost any more — there might even be a sale. And I'll bring your suit to be cleaned—' But here she bit her lip in dismay. 'I'd better not bring the suit; it might give me away,' she said.

'What about the parcels coming home?'

'Oh, I'll get them made up very small, or I'll get them sent by post — oh, I'll do something anyway; don't worry.' But she was a little bit worried herself. 'Maybe I ought to content myself with looking at the shop windows — or I might go out and get a breath of sea air. That was what Sam had in mind. He was always saying he wished I could get the taste of a good sea breeze — I'm sure that's what he'd wish I'd do. I didn't tell you, but I was dreaming of him last night; that's why I'm so sure he's dead. I forget what it was about — you know the way it is with dreams, they're so daft — but it was something to do with the sea. He must have been trying to put it into my head to go in the car! Sure he *must* be dead when he's able to put things in my way like that, don't you think? The Lord have mercy on him!'

It was a Saturday the car left for Dublin. According to Molly afterwards it was an uneasy car-load.

'Now before we start,' said the Sergeant, 'I want you

all to bear in mind that there are two purposes behind this trip. The first is to find the person in question, but the second purpose is to take particular note of the circumstances in which you find him.'

(You should have heard Molly taking him off for me afterwards.)

'I mean,' he went on, 'I mean that it is particularly important to the law to know if there is anything unusual, anything irregular, that is to say, in the behaviour of the said person. It can't be overlooked that this person might try on a certain trick he played before and the State cannot allow irresponsible people to be a source of expense and public disturbance.'

'You don't mean you'd have him committed?' cried Molly, with a gasp. It was all she could do not to say she was glad he was dead! 'Well, I hope you're not the one to find him, if that's what you'll be thinking about, instead of trying to make things easy for him. Or you either!' she said, turning her head to the fellow on the seat beside her, because who was he but another Garda, and she thought he had the same idea in mind as the Sergeant.

He had a face as long as a fast, this fellow.

'Ah, go easy on him, ma'am,' said the Sergeant. 'It's promotion he's after, poor fellow. He didn't know I was coming! He didn't tell me he was going either!'

'It's my day off,' said the young fellow sourly. 'I don't have to ask leave of anyone for what I do on my half-day.'

'Oh, so it's in a civilian capacity you came, is it?' said the Sergeant, and he gave another wink at Molly. 'Ah sure, I wronged you, man. In that case you wouldn't be eligible for promotion at all; but sure it's in heaven you'll get your reward. It's true to say it's hard to judge any man! Isn't that so, Captain?'

Because in spite of the Sergeant's efforts, the other two

people were still a sort of a dead-weight. The Captain
was one of the old gentry, and who was the other but
Miss Muggins, sister of the local member of the Dail,
that got into the Dail mainly because of a slogan he had
after the Troubles. 'We didn't go half far enough!'
That was the slogan. It meant we oughtn't to have left
the odd ninepin standing, like the Captain. The Sergeant
was uneasy between the two of them. Molly wasn't. Let
dog eat dog was her way of looking at them.

But the Captain was civil enough.

'Excuse me, Sergeant,' he said, 'but an interesting
point occurred to me. It's a matter of general interest
only, of course. But what is the position of a person that
is — what's this you said? — committed, is it? — in regard to his debts, I mean?'

The Sergeant sat up.

'Ah yes, Captain,' he said, 'but do you mean in regard
to money owed by the person to another person or persons,
or do you mean the money owed to this person by another
person or persons?'

That was the Sergeant's way of talking: it was to
bother people, maybe, but the Captain got his meaning all
right, and so did Molly. Molly, you see, knew all about
him owing Sam so much money because Sam told her.

It wasn't only for the saddles and things, but he'd got
a few more quid out of Sam from time to time by walking into the shop and asking for it, and telling Sam in a
lordly way to put it down on the bill. Oh, Molly knew
all about it.

'It's a pity,' said Sam to her one day, 'that the Captain
hasn't the income on all the money he owes me, because
then he could pay cash for everything to the end of his
days, and he'd need no more credit.'

Here was the puzzle: was the Captain hoping Sam
was alive or dead? Molly couldn't be sure. The talk
about committing the old fellow had him strayed.

'I'd have given anything if Sam could have seen him sitting there, looking like the rest of us for once in his life, instead of letting on he wasn't the same breed of bird at all, and it all only a matter of feathers.'

They were nearly in Dublin by this time.

'Where will we start?' said the Sergeant.

It was then that Miss Muggins came into the picture.

'If you've no objection, Sergeant, I know where I'll start! I don't know about the rest of you, but I'm not wasting any time looking in unlikely places!'

'Commendable, ma'am!' said the Sergeant. 'But I hope you haven't any special information that you failed to pass on to the proper quarters, by any chance?'

Miss Muggins drew herself up.

'I should think, Sergeant, that as my brother's sister you'd know that I would be fully aware of my duties in that and all matters of civic responsibility, but the knowledge I have is based entirely on what you might call my private insight into the character of this person.'

Now it was very hard on Molly to hear that one sitting there referring to Sam as This Person. She nearly lost her temper and said outright that it was no wonder he jilted her long ago — which was what everyone said. Only it wasn't really true. It was only people's talk, because there was never anything between them. Sam had told Molly all about it. Miss Muggins had something in for him all the same.

The Sergeant wasn't born yesterday, though.

'I'd have you know, ma'am,' he said sharply, 'we do a course of psychology in the Depot, and we take character into consideration too — at all times!'

He was having a dig at her there.

'Now, tell me this, ma'am. I seem to remember hearing that in a manner of speaking, you and this Person——?'

'Oh, that's what *he*'d like thought,' said Miss Mug-

gins. 'And I don't mind admitting that if it weren't
for certain things I discovered, we would have come to a
settlement without a doubt, because he was very persua-
sive, and he ought to have had a tidy sum in the bank if
it weren't —' and here she shot an unexpected glance at
the Captain — 'if it weren't for him being taken advantage
of by people.'

The Sergeant saw the glance.

'Ah, I think you have a spark of the old feeling for him
still, Miss Muggins,' he said, trying to be playful.

Miss Muggins wasn't one for playing.

'Not a spark!' she said. 'And what is more, I go down
on my knees every night and thank God for what I was
spared. Oh, women can be terribly deceived in a man.
There was everyone in the town linking our names, and
envying me, I'm sure, and the next thing they knew it
was all broken off, and no one knew the reason. Indeed,
there were some that were bad enough to think it was
broken off by him. If only they knew! But I am a con-
scientious woman, and I kept my lips sealed on what I
found out. I wasn't going to take away his character:
no matter what the cost to my own reputation.'

'Commendable, very commendable, ma'am,' said the
Sergeant again. 'Of course, there is a time and a place
for everything, and I suppose you feel that the present
circumstances are such that——'

'That's just what I felt, Sergeant. And I got my
brother to get me certain information.' She rummaged
in her bag and took out a piece of paper.

'May I see it, ma'am,' said the Sergeant, and he
stretched out. 'But it's only a list of streets,' he said, and
his face fell.

'That's all,' said Miss Muggins, with some asperity,
'but I think it ought to be your business, Sergeant, to
realize the kind of streets they are — unfortunate streets,
if I might say so! Unfortunate streets!'

Now you'd think my Molly wouldn't know what was meant, but she knew quicker than the Sergeant, and she was about to fly at the Muggins one !

'Easy now : easy,' said the Sergeant. 'We can neglect nothing, my dear, but perhaps we had better all separate and meet at the end of the day.'

'Put me down at the Pillar,' said Molly coldly, and left it at that.

Oh, but she had a great day. She got all the shopping done, and she managed to put on most of the things she bought, like as if she was going through the Customs, my pyjamas and the kids' vests, and I don't know what else. She must have looked a bit peculiar if you looked close, but sure no one saw her as things happened.

Because in spite of doing all the shopping, she kept it in mind to get that breath of sea-air that Sam was always talking about, and in the afternoon she hopped on a train and went off to Dunleary for a dander down the pier.

It wasn't as nice as it was in the morning. It was getting chilly. And the sun was a cold grudging sort of sun, and there was nobody on the pier. She thought she'd go out to the very end all the same, because it's nice out there the way they've sloped it off gradually so that the waves wash in across the flat stones like they do on the sand, not bashing against the rocks like they do at the sides of the pier. So on she went and the wind nearly dragging the clothes off her, till she came in sight of the end.

Well, there's no use making a mystery out of nothing ! Who did she see standing down at the edge of the water but Sam. The very one. But it was the way he was standing that got Molly. She didn't get time to think how odd it was him being there, because it was so odd the way he was standing. He was in his bare feet. Worse than that, he had taken off his pants and was standing there with nothing but his shirt on him. Do you know, the first thing Molly thought was that he was like the children when she'd be getting them ready for bed at night, and they'd run out on the landing, and start walking around, and them in no condition to appear before anyone but their mother.

Anyway, to cut things short, she ran up to him. She had him dressed again in jig-time, and no harm done.

'Were you out of your mind, Sam, to be standing like that?' she said. It was more of her way of saying the wrong thing at the right time.

'I suppose I was, Molly,' he said. 'I was thinking of how I used to paddle when I was a child.'

'Well, you're no child now, Sam,' said Molly. 'And what's more, you might go paddling on Sandymount Strand, or beyond at Dollymount, but you wouldn't paddle far out there.' She drew him back a bit more from the edge of the water. 'Don't you know it's deep enough there to take the mail-boat, and sometimes it comes in close enough to skin the lighthouse! Paddling indeed! If you didn't go straight to the bottom, Sam, you'd be taken up and put into an asylum. How would you like that?'

'Oh, I wouldn't like that at all, Molly,' said the poor old fellow, and he started to cry. 'Do you know, that's what I'm always thinking will happen to me in the end. When I'm sitting in the shop all alone, I often wonder what will be the end of me.'

'God help him. It would break your heart,' said Molly. 'Sure you'd have to do something for him.'

'Come on out of that, Sam,' she said. 'I know what will be the end of you. And there'll be no more living alone either. Sure God never meant any of us to be alone till we're boxed up in our coffins. Haven't we plenty of room for you, and you can pay us a few shillings so as not to feel under a compliment to us! How would you like that?'

He liked it well, I needn't tell you. And it wasn't for long anyway, God help him.

We didn't lose by it either, except that the Sergeant had his nose in the air for a while, and the others were lepping mad. Because Molly didn't go back to the Pillar at all, and the car — with the lot of them sitting in it — was there till nearly midnight waiting for her. She went home on the train. Sam had plenty of money in his pocket. You should have seen the cakes and buns they brought with them!

We all had a share in the day, you might say.

There was only one cloud for Molly. She left her hat behind her on the pier; I suppose it floated off on the waves, like the Garda's hat floated over the weir, only there was no one to give it a cheer. It was a new hat, too.

'Ah well — it didn't suit me anyway,' she said.

Didn't suit her? And she only after buying it! What I sometimes wonder is, will I ever understand her; my Molly?

Loving Memory

'THE child of a ghost — who'd marry me!' cried Alice. She was fifteen then, but years before that she knew she'd never marry — years before her mother died she knew it. They were branded even then — the love-birds' children!

'Now for the love-birds' tray,' old Ellen used to say, after she'd given them their meal. She'd heave a sigh and get to her feet.

There was a fiction kept up in the house that it was only their mother who had her meals brought upstairs, but their father was always nipping into the china-cupboard and taking down a cup and saucer. 'Put mine on the tray too, Ellen. I have a few things I want to say to my wife.'

'You'd think they'd get enough of each other sometime or other, wouldn't you?' Ellen would grumble, as she steadied the tray on her knee at the foot of the big dark stairway. 'Love-birds; a pair of love-birds.'

'Does that mean we are love-children?' Alice asked earnestly one day. Alice was the oldest. She was nine then.

Ellen gave a big laugh. 'If they heard that!' she cried. 'Where did you learn the like? Do you know what it means?' She laughed again, and then she looked soberly at them. 'You're no such thing,' she said. 'No such thing.'

The children looked at each other. Were they something still more odd?

'Ah, don't worry your heads, children,' said Ellen kindly. 'Love is the same as anything else in the world: it's all right in its own place — *and* in moderation.'

They knew. Overhead they could hear their mother's

feet tapping back and forth across her room. If only she
didn't hog it all: the love, they meant.

'There are some houses,' said Ellen, 'and the love is
thrown about like a thing of no value at all. But never
mind,' she added consolingly, 'houses like that are very
untidy — *very* untidy.' The children nodded. They
knew. Their house wasn't littered with love.

'— and noisy,' said Ellen.

They knew. Love didn't thunder like a cataract down
their staircase. It was all kept stored in their mother's
room, and only their father had the key.

'And to think,' cried Ellen, 'that when he was a young
fellow, no one thought he'd ever marry, much less take to
it like another man would take to drink.'

It was a fact that when he was a young fellow Mathias
Grimes was so shy of love he was a reproach to the town,
for it was a great town for love — in its way. And the
Grimes' parlour was what you might call the Temple of
that love. For Mathias had two sisters, and they were a
great draw. Their father was dead and their old mother
was bedridden for so long the girls had their own way in
everything and no interference. They were both good-
looking girls too, and Nell had a lovely touch on the
piano. Minnie had a voice, or at least an ear. From the
street you'd think it was a dance hall to hear the laughing
and the singing and the thumping on the keyboard:

> I love you and *you* love me,
> I'm for you, and *you*'re for me.

The two Grimes girls were older than Mathias, even
Minnie the younger one was a good eight or nine
years older than him, but they looked like two school-
girls, the way they wore their hair looped down over one
shoulder so girlishly. All the same, they were a long time
about getting married. But that was the great thing
about the parlour. There was no knowing what a word

could do, or where it might lead. And no one had to
plough a single furrow. Courtship was a sort of co-
operative effort.

'Oh, I'm sorry, Eddy,' a girl might cry, over-emphatic-
ally, if her loop of hair brushed into a fellow's face when
she bent to turn a sheet of music.

'No need to be so sorry, Nell! I'm sure he loved it —
isn't that so, Eddy?'

And what would Eddy say? It hardly mattered. One
word was enough to send innuendoes echoing through the
evening.

'Do it again, Nell, till we see how he likes it!'

Lightly, loosely, couples were linked together till a
fine mesh of compromise was woven around them.

'Your hair is nice tonight, Minnie — what did you do
to it?'

'My hair! It's a show! It's always awful when I
wash it — it's far too thick!'

The convention that hair was too long, too thick, or
too silky — skin too fine, too delicate, was never accepted
by the men.

'Oh, come now, you're looking for compliments.'

'From whom, I'd like to know? Not you!'

'And why not — do you think I'm no good at that
kind of thing?'

'It's not a question of being good at it — it's a question
of——'

'— of what?'

'— of the consequences!'

'Oh, so that's it — you think I'm afraid of the consequences. Well — suppose you were mistaken about that?'

'But I'm not!'

'I wouldn't be so sure if I were you!'

Meaningless, idle, leading nowhere, the banter went
on inconsequentially until, almost by a slip of the tongue,
a remark more pointed than the usual would be acclaimed

as a kind of a public proposal. Then, but not till then, could a couple claim the prize of the parlour; the right to sit on the sofa behind the parlour door.

This sofa was really only an outsize armchair, big enough for two people. Its particularity lay in the fact that whenever the parlour door was opened or shut — even for a minute — the sofa went into total eclipse.

Only a hug at most, or a squeeze, would be covered by this eclipse, but it was enough to stop the piano and turn the singing into whistling and cat-calling.

In a way that nook behind the door was a symbol of love as understood by the town. The nearer a couple got to marriage the more they were given cover, till finally marriage itself came down like a snuffer over their flame.

It was on this point, as to where love got private, that Mathias fell foul of the town. He had always been awkward as a boy. He had been sent away to school more to get him out of the way than anything else, until he was old enough to take over the business, which was kept going by the sisters. When he came back from Newbridge, however, he seemed more awkward than ever. He couldn't be got into the parlour for all the tea in China. And one evening, when his sisters and their friends tried, for a dare, to drag him in there, it's certain he'd have got away naked if they hadn't let go of him before the clothes parted from him.

He used to spend the afternoons and evenings mooning about the ramparts that ran brokenly round the town. These ramparts dated from King John's visit to Ireland, but for years they had been put to practical use as boundary walls for the business premises and the old family residences that made up the town proper. These old premises all had big wild gardens at the back, and of them all the Grimes' garden was wildest and most over-grown. It was used only for tossed out crates and cardboard cartons from the packing house, and actually these did

not look as bad as might be thought, they were so quickly
grown through and grown over by nettles and other
weeds.   Sticking up among the spiked nettles away at the
far end of the garden was a butt of a tower that had once
been a watch tower on the rampart.   Here Mathias often
sat for hours.   A flight of broken steps led up to the tower
from the inside, and there was a drop of fifty feet on the
outer side, so that it was like a belvedere or gazebo for
viewing the countryside.

It wasn't much of a view.   Nothing but flat fields of
thin grass stretched away to all sides, marred at many
points by ugly concrete bungalows.   These bungalows
were held in great contempt by the Grimes girls.   Because
of the size of the Grimes' premises which had originally
comprised three separate buildings, it was not unreason-
able for Nell and Minnie to expect that the partitions that
had been knocked down by their grandfather could be
put up again by Mathias to provide accommodation for
them if need arose.   This would widen the field of eligibles
for them, and take in bank clerks, government officials,
and insurance inspectors with fair salaries but no houses,
residing as they were forced to do in the Central Hotel.
After all, a small part of the house would do for Mathias.
The part occupied by the old lady would do nicely for
him when she passed away.

For it was somehow assumed he would remain a
bachelor, although at this time Mathias was only in his
early twenties.   Apparently, however, it was only of
love's preliminaries that Mathias was shy, for in the spring
of his twenty-fourth year, and no more than one month
after the old lady died, Mathias had not only met someone to his liking, but within two weeks had asked her to
marry him.   Further still, he had named the day of the
wedding, a date which gave him exactly six weeks to
make and carry out his plans.

He had had a touch of bronchitis after the funeral and

had been persuaded to go to the Spa Hotel in Lisdoon-
varna. He stayed away only four days as there was a
commercial traveller he wanted to see on the fourth day,
but the following Sunday he hired a car and drove over
there again. The Sunday after that he hired the car again.
Then, just as his astonished sisters were beginning to smell
a rat he broke the news to them. He told them his plans:
his plans for them. He had bought them one of the new
bungalows outside the town, and he expected them to
install themselves in it before the wedding.

That night there was such consternation in the parlour
that there wasn't a single note struck on the piano.

'But what is she like? Do you mean to say you never
saw her?'

'And her name? You've told us nothing!'

Nell and Minnie hardly knew her name.

'He speaks of her as Alicia,' said Nell doubtfully. 'It's
a form of Alice, I think.'

'Then why isn't she called Alice, I wonder?'

The sisters didn't know.

'I always think Alice sounds a bit youngish,' said Minnie.

'But isn't she young?' they all cried.

'Oh, I suppose she must be,' said Minnie, but somehow vague doubts about the bride had formed in everyone's mind.

'Oh, well, we'll soon see her, I suppose,' said Eddy
Troddyn. 'When is he bringing her over here? You'll
have to meet her before the wedding.'

A day or two later, however, Mathias announced that
he was not bringing Alicia home until after the wedding.

'After they're *married*? What good will that be?' cried
the crowd. 'All the fun will be over then!'

Not a cuddle, not a squeeze would anyone have seen.
Cold fish that he was, no better might have been expected
from Mathias. But what of the girl? Had she no spark
at all in her?

Could she be older than him? Could it have been a made-match? No one ever denied he was eligible.

'I bet she's years older than him!'

The girls were more disparaging than the men. The men were inclined to look on Mathias with a new respectful curiosity.

'She may be a good business woman — and she may have a bit of money too.'

She had no money, though. Nell could tell them that. Six weeks from the day they met, Alicia was to have gone out to America to an aunt of hers, who had sent her the passage money. Mathias made her send back the money, and the day named for the wedding was the day she was to have sailed, because she had given notice for the day before that in the millinery where she worked.

'She can't be so old at all. They only want young girls in America.'

'Wait a minute: I've an idea!' cried Eddy Troddyn. 'Where are they going for the honeymoon? If she's old it will be Dublin. If she has a jog in her at all it will be Tramore or Kilkee!'

For the really incomprehensible news had not been divulged. 'I didn't tell you,' said Nell, flushing, 'but he says they're not having any honeymoon.'

'Nell! Are you raving?' There was pandemonium. 'You're joking!'

Nell and Minnie were not joking. It was no joke at all to get rid of the rubbish of years in six weeks, and pack into a box of a bungalow. A honeymoon would at least have given them a bit more time. As it was they had only a few days left. Oh, that bungalow! Their only hope was that they might not be long in it, but the coming of the bride to the house in the market square gave to the whole removal a touch of dowagerdom.

'If you ask me,' said Nell, 'she can't wait to get her hand into the till!'

Grasping? That could be another explanation. Elderly? Ailing? Money-grubbing? There was no end to the speculations about Alicia. Starting straight into marriage without a honeymoon was like starting into Lent without Shrove Tuesday. It would be good-bye to the fun in the parlour!

'We'll miss these nights at the piano,' said Eddy.

'You'll be more than welcome in the bungalow,' said Minnie.

'If only it wasn't so far out from the town,' wailed Eddy, '— and is it true you won't have the piano? We heard it wouldn't fit into the bungalow. Is that so?'

It was so. A sadness fell on the room. It was hard to think that all the swaying and singing around the old piano was already nearly a thing of the past. And each evening the sadness deepened till the last evening of all came round.

That last evening a real effort was made to be light-hearted. It was only when everyone was out on the pavement going home, however, and the door was safely shut on the Grimes' household that the one really good laugh of the evening was raised. 'I forgot to tell you all — I know the bride's secret,' said Eddy. Putting out his arms he drew them all into a ring. 'She has a wooden leg,' he whispered.

They had to run away up the street so as not to let the laughing be heard by those inside.

And yet it was well they had a bit of fun that night because there was a kind of embarrassment over all the town the next night. The Grimes sisters came home from the wedding on the afternoon train but they went straight out to the bungalow. The bridal pair were not coming till the late train. Now, apart from the evenings in the Grimes' parlour, the only regular pastime in the town was going down to the station to see the late train pass through, and maybe get an evening paper from the stoker or the guard. It didn't seem nice, however, to go down that evening.

So there wasn't a soul on the platform when Mathias and Alicia stepped off the train. It was a fine night, but the moon had not risen, and the streets were dark. They encountered no one as they walked up from the station to the Market Square. And the house, when they came in sight of it, was dark, because Mathias had given orders that no lamps were to be lit in the parlour. 'I hate that parlour, Ellen,' he said vehemently. 'I'm going to speak to a contractor and see about having it let in with the shop.'

'Very good, sir,' said Ellen, but it flustered her, and she wondered if she was to prepare the big parlour upstairs that had never been used in her time except for rooting geranium slips.

'Oh, no need: no need,' said Mathias. 'A fire in the bedroom will be enough: we'll be tired out.'

The flicker of this fire on the ceiling was, therefore, all the light that could be seen from the old house as Mathias unlinked his arm from Alicia to let them inside with his own key. Ellen hadn't heard them coming. She didn't even know they had arrived and gone upstairs until her niece told her. The niece had seen the light in the big oblong window upstairs as she was coming down the street to see if Ellen needed a hand. As she got nearer to the house indeed the window got brighter and brighter, as if one after another every lamp in the house had been carried into the room. There was never such illumination in the Market Square, and although the blind was drawn, there was a golden oblong larger than life traced out on the street below.

'How did they get in without my hearing?' cried Ellen, rushing towards the stairs. But Mathias was half-way down.

'Can I have a glass of milk, Ellen?' he asked timidly.

'Is it for yourself?' said Ellen, taken aback.

'No. For her,' said Mathias.

'But surely she's going to have something more sub-
stantial than that after the journey?'

'We had a meal on the train,' said Mathias. 'We're
not hungry. If you give me the glass of milk I'll take it
up to her, Ellen.'

'Am I not going to see her at all?' cried Ellen.

'Tomorrow,' said Mathias gently, and he smiled as he
took the milk from her and went back up the stairs.

Ellen turned to the niece.

'There must be some truth in what was said about her,'
she said dejectedly. 'She must be older than him — a
lot older!'

'Oh, I wouldn't say that!' cried the girl. 'I didn't
tell you, but I saw her shadow on the window-blind when
I was coming down the street, and it wasn't an old-
looking shadow at all.'

It was, in fact, a very young shadow. And it darted
like quicksilver over the blind, while, down in the street
below, at wing with it, went the shadow of the shadow,
and it looked so agile and living a thing that the heart
would flinch to step on it.

Before the couple were home ten minutes, everyone in
the town had stolen a glance at that oblong window. It
stayed lit up for about twenty minutes more, and then it
went dark. Rebuked, those who were looking up, looked
down. But not for long. With a pinging sound that was
heard all over the Square, the ivory knob at the end of
the blind-cord spanked against the window-pane and the
blind was let slap up again. Then, with a rattle of dry
putty the big window sash was thrown up also and a
young woman put out her head.

'Oh, such a night!' she cried loudly and youngly.
'Come and see, Mathias!' And leaning her elbows out
on the sill, she waited for him to come and lean out with

her. Together they contemplated the night for all the
world as if they were on a balcony in some distant
Italian resort.

Now this was not what the town had been led to expect.
They had been told there would be no honeymoon — not
that it was to be spent brazenly before their eyes in their
own town. After all, it is not only the couple concerned
that a honeymoon safeguards! Friends, relations, and
acquaintances are entitled to a like protection.

As the night wore on, however, the oblong window,
lit or unlit, magnetized the town. It could only be hoped
that daylight would bring the couple to a sense of decorum.

The next day was a Sunday.

'Well, Ellen?' asked Nell and Minnie, as they met on
the way to Mass. (It was a fine day, and it was a nice
walk in from the bungalow, but how would it be on a
wet day?) Ellen pursed her lips. 'Breakfast in bed!'
she said cryptically. 'I hope that won't be kept up for long.'

'For her, of course?'

'For both of them,' said Ellen, 'sitting up together
like a King and a Queen!'

A few paces further along the street Ellen met with
more enquiries.

'She's young after all, I hear? How about her looks?'

Ellen could not deny that the bride had looks. 'Take
care but she's too good-looking, though!' she said. 'I
found out one thing. It was her doing they didn't go
away on any honeymoon. She told me when I went up
with the tray — straight out in front of him, too. She
said she wanted to spend her first night in their own—'
she faltered. 'I'll spell it,' she conceded, 'in their own
b-e-d! There!'

It was felt by Ellen — it was felt by all — to be, at the
least, an *unnecessary* remark.

Then, just in time for late Mass — Mathias and Alicia
appeared in the street — linked. Linked they went up the

street.   And only to take holy water and genuflect did they
unlink.

'It's a wonder she didn't link him all during Mass !'

'It was bad enough the way they kneeled so close up
to one another !'

But it was those in the gallery had a really good view
of them.   'Do you know where she had her hand?   In
his pocket !'

Clearly there was going to be a scandal.   It was scandal enough to think that he was not going to let her set
foot in the shop.   Who did he think she was — the Queen
of Sheba ?   He'd soon change that tune.

But on Monday morning the contractor started breaking down the wall between the parlour and the shop, and
not only was Alicia kept out of the shop but she had to
spend most of her day out of sight upstairs.   From the
start this gave her a remote air, like a lady in a tower.
But if Alicia spent her day up in her tower, Mathias spent
the best part of his day on the stairs, going up or coming
down.   The only time they were seen downstairs was
when they came down to go out for their walk, which,
wet or fine, they took every day of the year.

Those walks !   Linked like lovers, every afternoon they
sailed off out of the town and round the rampart-walls,
seemingly aware of none but themselves.

'There's only one thing will put a stop to their gallop,'
said Ellen.   'One of these days she'll learn there are more
uses than one for a bed.'   Ellen was sick and tired of
bringing up meals to that bedroom.

But four births, and two miscarriages, took place in
the big bridal bed, and for Mathias, Alicia emerged from
them more precious than ever.

None of her children was like her.   Fragments of her
charm, particles of her enchantment had been scattered
among them.   The eyes of one, the hair of another might
occasionally be remarked upon, but no one of them could

ever have held a candle to her. Every year Mathias got more insistent that she keep to her room and rest.

'Put another cup on the tray, Ellen,' he'd say, as he dodged in from the shop, and put his foot to the stairs.

'Nothing at all about me lugging these heavy trays up there!' said Ellen grumpily. 'You'd think she'd get tired of looking at the one wallpaper all day long.'

Ellen had a name for that room. She called it the love-nest.

Alicia somehow suggested bird images all the time. She was given to wearing bird feathers, as it happened. She had a hat with a blue quill that quivered when she walked. And she had another with the whole wing of a bird, not only the stiff fan feathers but the little bone that bends back, like an elbow, plumed with down. Above all, there was her secret urge to fly up to her room all the time, as a bird returns unremittingly to its nest.

Poor bird: she never made her nest in the heart of her children; that is certain. Any afternoon they could be seen upstairs in the big parlour standing at the window when Alicia and Mathias were setting out for their famous afternoon walk.

Mathias and Alicia were never late. At four o'clock exactly the door opened and they stepped into the street. There was a short delay, while Mathias turned to shut the door, and Alicia caught back the small brown muff she wore on a silver chain around her neck, and that dangled out from her seeming to draw them apart. Then Mathias shoved his outer hand into his outer pocket, and with the other linked Alicia fast. Her free hand she pushed into the muff, and by pressing closer to him she was able to push in also the arm he held. But because the big granite sill of the upstairs window was as broad as a parapet, these preliminaries were all but hidden from the children. For them there was, about the pair below, and the way they stepped off the kerb, a precipitancy that

could only be compared with the way the swallow leaves
the eave. With but an instant's effort, they seemed to
leave one element and effortlessly enter another, even
more familiar.

Off they went then up the street, while Alicia's muff
that now hung down between them seemed to hold them
tight like an iron padlock. That muff — when seen like
that from a distance — had the solidest look. Yet, when
they came back, and Alicia took the chain from around
her neck and laid the little muff on the table in the hall,
it was seen in all its frailty. It was not made of any
sturdy fur, but hundreds of maribou feathers so soft and
light that for a long time after she laid it down it trembled
like a living thing.

'Come and put away Alicia's muff,' Mathias would
order the children, for the muff was kept down in the
hall in a special box, like a pet.

It was always as Alicia that he spoke of her, even to
the children. They could not recall a single time that he
called her Mother except the one day they came back
early from their walk.

The children weren't expecting them, and weren't
at the window. They only heard the voices down in the
hall, their father's and Ellen's. They ran and looked
down the well of the stairs. It was when he looked up
and saw them that Mathias dropped the Alicia.

'Your mother isn't well,' he cried. 'Come down and
carry up her things.'

For Ellen had taken off their mother's coat, and her
shoes. She was only in her blouse. And she had been
put sitting on a chair in the hall: not the hard oak chair
that was always there but an old wicker chair out of the
kitchen. Her head was thrown back. From the stair-
head a cold north light poured down, and lay whitely on
her face and on her hair that glistened with sweat.

But before the children got down, Ellen and Mathias

had decided to try and get her up the stairs, and so the children were right in their way.

'Out of the way — out of the way,' cried Mathias, and, terrified of his voice, they stitched themselves to the wall.

'Wait! Let me breathe. Let me rest,' said Alicia weakly, in a whisper, and at the same time her beautiful eyes rested on them. 'Speak gently — to them,' she said, with an effort, and before she attempted another step she looked at them again fixedly. Then she closed her eyes with the effort of taking the step upward, and from her wet hair sweat ran down her face like tears.

Then she opened her eyes again, very wide.

'My muff —' she said, each word distinct, 'don't — let it — get stepped on — in the — fuss.'

The fuss was near an end, whether she knew it or not — whether Mathias did; or Ellen.

'How will he live without her?' That was the question everyone asked when word went round that she was dying. And even on the day of the funeral concern was centred on him. No one took any notice of the children as they stood around the grave, up to their necks in black. How would he take it? He'd start to drink. He'd go out of his mind. He'd follow her to the grave within the year!

'The children won't be any consolation to him,' said Ellen openly in front of them. 'He'd have seen them all put down if it could have saved her!'

Yet Mathias actually took it fairly well in the beginning. After the funeral he let himself be led out of the cemetery willingly enough. But the truth may have been that he had in his head, even then, the idea that was to sustain him. That night he went up to the parlour where the children were all gathered together not knowing what to do. He had an armful of catalogues and leaflets in his hands. 'You're not too young,' he said, stiffly and formally, 'to help me choose a fitting memorial for her. Come here, please.'

They gathered eagerly around him. It was a relief to have something to do. To the smaller ones it was as good as a game to go through the pictures of tombs and headstones.

'Oh, look at this one, Father!'

'Too big — too vulgar-looking!' said Mathias.

'There's a nice one, Father — with doves!'

'Too small — too insignificant. And not enough room for the inscription.'

By bedtime they hadn't settled on anything.

'Not that there's any great hurry,' said Mathias, as he put away the catalogues. 'Better be sure than sorry.'

The next night they went over the catalogues again. He found nothing to his satisfaction, however. The night after that they had several new catalogues that he had had sent by post. Scrolls, crosses, urns, tablets: every kind of shape was considered. 'Nothing worthy of her!' he cried in despair. 'Nothing to do justice to her. We must get something striking. I want something that will catch the eye the moment people enter the cemetery. In that way we'll make sure she isn't forgotten. Even people who did not know her will ask who she was and want to know all about her.'

The thought of erecting a really striking memorial gave him such pleasure; it didn't seem to matter that he couldn't find a suitable one.

'Did you think of a Pietà, Father?'

'Too impersonal!'

'A weeping angel?'

'Only for infants.'

'Oh, I know, Father,' cried Alice one day. 'How about a stone casket?'

He seemed to like that idea, and his face lit up for a minute, but then he shook his head. She couldn't help feeling sorry for him when he gave his reason.

'It would be very heavy over her,' he said.

In fact, he was beginning to despair of the catalogues.

'I think I'll walk down to the cemetery,' he said to Alice. 'I might get an idea walking around and looking at the graves.'

It seemed a good idea. He was pale from sticking in the house. He missed his afternoon walks with Alicia.

Alice ran to get his hat and coat.

'It'll be a nice walk for you, Father.'

He looked better, too, when he came back. She was glad to see he had more colour in his face, and more life in him.

'It was a good thing I went down there,' he said. 'There's something we hadn't thought of at all — the amazing way in which different materials withstand the weather. I didn't know marble was so easily stained! After a few years it's yellow and streaky. I think we may rule out marble!' he said decisively. 'That leaves only limestone and granite. Now granite I know is excellent on a fine day; the mica sparkles in the sunlight. But I wonder how it stands up to rain?' He glanced at the barometer. 'If it's wet tomorrow I'll go down there again and take a walk around. I'd like to see what effect the rain has on it.'

'But people don't visit the cemetery on a wet day,' said Alice.

'What about the day of the funeral?' he asked. 'Funerals are not postponed for a shower. And when people are there, they look around them and cannot avoid seeing what's to be seen. Let's hope there will be a shower tomorrow.'

It was downright wet next day. Mathias went off early with his umbrella.

Granite was ruled out when he came back.

'And I'll tell you another thing,' he said animatedly, as Alice helped him out of his wet clothing. 'I have to acknowledge that limestone can look very depressing in the rain. It gets a very dark, saturated appearance. I must admit that marble comes off best in the wet. Rain gives it a great gloss. Yes; there's a lot more to be said for marble than I thought at first. And one mustn't forget that it can be re-polished if it gets stained! We must remember that in its favour,' he said warmly.

He was greatly exhilarated.

Then there was another day when he left for the cemetery early in the afternoon, only to return hastily after a few minutes or so.

'Have you got a tape-measure, Alice?' he asked. 'I've just realized one must have a proper proportion between the stone and the plot. This is a science in itself, you see,' he said importantly, as he set off once more. He came back in high spirits. 'I'm glad I thought of that nicety,' he said, giving back the tape. 'Her grave will never be completely cast into shade by the stone!'

It was a nicety indeed. Alice could hardly appreciate it. Yet finer niceties still were to be considered.

'I wonder if shadows cast by the moon are the same length as those cast in sunlight?' he asked her suddenly one evening.

'Oh, Father! The cemetery is locked at sundown,' she cried.

'Not locked,' he said gently. 'The gates are only closed over.'

Alice knew then that he'd been down there some of the evenings when she'd thought he'd gone around the ramparts. She began to worry vaguely then — about him only, of course. It wasn't as if Alicia was only a few days dead. The weeks were passing, and the months. If in the start he had gone more often than was wise, he might by now have been going less often. The opposite, however, was the case. This was a passion that was taking possession of him. Like love, it seemed to grow without diminish.

'Stay at home for once, Father,' cried Alice. 'Don't go down there this evening.'

'But look at the night it is,' he cried; 'a beautiful night for a walk, and later there will be a moon, and I can measure the shadows on the grave.'

'Then I'll come with you,' she said.

'Not *with* me — I can't be delayed —' Alice felt helpless. 'After me if you like,' he murmured, slippery, slyly, and was out the door before she could get her coat.

It was a few minutes before Alice was ready to follow him. He was right about the night. It was good to be out on such a night. It was what was called a "pet" evening, that is to say, it was not summer, but late spring, and yet a softness and warmth had come in the air that was unexpected so early in the year. It was already dusk, but a number of small stars could be seen if you peered into the heavens. They were not the hard white stars that sharpen a sky, but a vague scattering of little lights, soft and warm, that looked as if they belonged to a human world.

Because it was such a pet evening, children were still playing in the streets, and although now and then a woman might come to an open doorway as if of a mind to call them inside, she hesitated, and she only looked out bemused, unwilling to grudge them the last vestiges of the magic moments.

Down near the cemetery there were a lot of children. It seemed late for them to be out, because the road near there was dark with high trees. As Alice went nearer, she could hear their high-pitched voices, and when she got close, she saw they had climbed upon the cemetery railings and were sticking their heads between the bars. They were chanting some silly song.

When they heard her coming they stopped. And she thought that when they saw who it was they jumped down sheepishly from the railings. They fell so silent, the silence was as silly as their silly singing.

'Is my father inside?' she asked on an impulse.

The question acted like magic to free their tongues.

'He's over there, miss. Beside the grave,' they cried.

They were all willingness, all helpfulness, all eagerness. One of them rushed to open the gate for her.

'Would you like us to go in with you, miss?'

She remembered that unaccompanied children were never allowed into the cemetery. They wanted a chance to get in there.

'Oh, no,' she cried. 'I've only come to fetch home my father,' she said.

They nodded their heads sagaciously. When she went to pass through the gateway, though, they still blocked her way. And when they asked her another question, she couldn't tell at the time if it was asked slyly or innocently.

'Who does he be talking to in there, miss?' they asked.

Alice hesitated.

'Himself, I suppose,' she said, trying to be frank with them, but she saw they received her explanation dubiously. 'You should be at home at this hour!' she said, rasped. 'Your mothers will be looking for you.'

There was indeed someone calling at that moment, further down the road.

'Child-ren!' said the voice. 'Child-ren!'

It carried well, that voice, like a coin tossed into the air, an unrelated thing, inconsequent, like the cuckoo's call.

Alice listened for a minute, and then went into the brightness of the cemetery. Roots were troublesome when a grave was being dug, so there were no trees in the cemetery, but even without the light of the moon there was a whiteness everywhere, of marble slabs and ornaments.

'Father, you must come home,' she called to him.

'You're carrying this thing too far. You can't make her live for ever, no matter what you do. And after all, she was only an ordinary woman. She wasn't an Egyptian queen!'

She was harsh and bitter. Yet he, when he answered her, was so gentle and conciliatory.

'For ever is a long time indeed,' he said sedately. 'But I know she'd like to be remembered as long as possible! Don't wait for me! I'm watching for the moon to shine out full. I have a few more measurements to take.'

Alice stood irresolute.

And then the moon shone out. Trees by the gate threw one great mass of shadow over half the graveyard, but at the edge the shadow was serrated. Each young leaf cut out its own sharp shape. And she could count every pebble of the gravel. Here and there a pebble, larger than the others, cast a pebble of shadow, and the path was dappled.

Then the woman's voice called out again as she stood there, the woman away in the dark, and Alice in the light.

'Child-ren — child-ren!'

The young girl waited. The voice fell to earth. Then, after a minute it came again, but nearer, and now it was a purely human voice.

'Children? Where are you?'

Was there a giggle in the dark high grass inside the gate?

'I hear you. I know you're there. Come along home at once. You'll answer for this! Don't make me come and get you. Do you think I don't see you?'

The last feint was so feeble, even to the woman herself, that in another minute she raised her voice again in a high, timeless note.

'Child-ren! Child-ren!'

The giggling this time was ill-concealed; and some-where near, a fat bottom flopped backwards into the moist grasses.

'Oh, you devils,' cried the woman. 'Stay out all night if you like! But you know what'll happen?'

Alice thought she knew, too. She waited for the age-old threat by which Ellen had got herself and her sisters and brothers in from the dark corners of the garden. When all other threats had failed, Ellen used to warn them that Mad Mary would get them. Who was Mad Mary? Was she a real person? Or was there a Mad Mary in every town, a puppet in the prop-box of bogeys and bugbears with which exasperated parents scarified their offspring when they themselves were at the end of their own nervous energy? She smiled.

And so she was actually smiling when the threat was finally flung out.

'Stay, so — ' the woman said, 'and see what'll happen! Have you forgotten Alicia Grimes? Oh-ho, you haven't! Alicia Grimes will get you! Alicia Grimes will get you!'

The Yellow Beret

'MAYBE it's the same one,' said Mag.

'*How* could it be the same?' cried Don. 'Wasn't the other one down at the docks? Do you never look at the papers?'

'But two murders in the one night!' Mag knew the note of doubt in her voice would annoy him, but she couldn't help it.

To please him, she peered across the breakfast table at the paper in his hand, but without her glasses the sun made one of everything on the table — plates, napery, and newsprint. And waywardly too her mind swayed away from it all, and went back to her own concerns. She'd soon have to call Donny. She glanced to see if his entrance card for his examination was still propped in front of the clock, so he couldn't possibly forget it when he was going out. She looked around the room to make sure there was nothing else he was likely to forget — his fountain pen, or the key of his locker in College.

But all the time, however, she felt Don was critical of her lack of attention.

'I hope we're not going to have a wave of crime!' she said.

Exactly the wrong thing to say. She had only revealed the full extent of her heedlessness.

'Wave of crime!' he scoffed. 'I told you there was no connection between the two crimes. You're as bad as the newspapers,' he said, irritated. But as he read on he became more amiable. 'I admit it's a disturbing business,' he conceded. 'It will have a very upsetting effect on people, I'm afraid!'

Well, here was something Mag could discuss with a genuine interest and liveliness.

'I don't see why!' she cried. 'I don't see why anyone should be upset — ordinary people, I mean — there's always a reason for these murders! Don't tell me they come out of a clear sky! I see no reason why people should be concerned at all about them — beyond feeling sorry for those involved, of course! Take that girl at the docks. I'm sure what happened to her was only the end of a long story!'

'Not necessarily,' said Don curtly. 'As a matter of fact they're looking for a Dutch sailor who only went ashore a few hours before the murder——'

' —but he knew her from another time, I suppose, and——'

'Not necessarily,' said Don again.

Mag reddened. She hadn't understood that it might all have happened in that doorway, not only the murder, but . . . well . . . it all.

'Oh!' she said slowly, repulsed, and then her voice quickened. 'Oh, Don,' she cried, 'let's not talk about it. Let's not even think about it. You know how I feel about that kind of thing.'

It was not so much a feeling as an attitude. She had always made it a point to draw a circle, as it were, around the home, and keep out all talk of such things. She had always tried to let the boys feel they lived in a totally different world from the world where such things happened. Don't talk about it. Don't think about it. That was her counsel to herself as well as to them.

It wasn't as easy to practise as to preach, though. Last night she had only caught a word or two about that girl who was strangled on the docks, and yet she could not get the thing out of her mind all night. Although she had never been out to the Pigeon House where it happened, and had only seen the long sea wall from the deck of the B. & I. Boat — seen it sliding past as the steamship pulled out into the Alexandra Basin — yet her mind kept picturing the scene as if it were a place she knew well.

Through the cranes and ships' rigging, she had seen the wide wharf narrow into a place with no human habitations; nothing but coal-yards, and warehouse yards, and the Power Station of Pigeon House itself, its windows lit by day as well as night with a cold inimical light. Then it narrowed again until it seemed only a promenade for birds, bollarded here and there, and splattered with glaring white droppings. The steps that led down from it into the water seemed senseless, more than half of them always under water, wobbly-looking and pale, while sometimes a wash of water, thin as ice, lay over the top step.

It was there she pictured it happening. Not at the edge near the sea-steps, but where, in an abortive bit of wall, an iron gate stood giving entrance or egress to nowhere. She saw the gate distinctly. It was reinforced top and bottom with rusty corrugated iron that had been cut in jags along the top as if with giant pinking shears.

How could a place she had never seen be so vivid in her mind? Even then, in the sunny breakfast-room, with terror she felt the picture forming once more in her mind. But this time there was a man in the picture. It was him: the murderer. Who else could it be?

Bending downward, in the gateway, but with his back to her she saw him, too, as clearly as she saw the place he stood. His clothes — a faded blue shirt — his hair — a carroty red — were as plain as if he were in front of her in the flesh. A feeling of gratefulness that she could not see his face had hardly passed over her till it was followed by the knowledge that in a minute he would straighten up and turn around. He would have to turn. For him — if it was him — and who else could it be —

that Dutch sailor — there was no going further down the sea wall. He would have to get back to peopled places. And she would be forced to see him face to face. And when she saw his face — ah, this was the terror — it would be, she felt certain, a face that was known to her.

What was the meaning of it? There was never anything psychic about her.

Desperately she closed her eyes to blot it all out — the gateway, the figure, but against her closed lids they formed again; more clearly. And then — as she knew he must — the man turned, or half-turned rather, because only his eyes turned towards her; his face and head remained partly averted. His head indeed, seemed fixed in an implacable pose as if it had no power to move, and yet in another sense it was all movement. Within itself as it were there was a terrible motion. Every cell of skin and hair and membrane seemed to vibrate. The coarse orange hair quivered, and the fibrous beard, while the enormous white whorl of the one ear visible seemed as if evolving still from its first convolution. And not only the face but the very air seemed to whirl and spin until it, too, became all spirals and oscillations. She was rigid with tension.

But the white whorl of that ear brought her suddenly to her senses. Van Gogh! The self-portrait! Relief left her so limp she slumped down in her chair. She glanced at Don. What a fool she was!

Why *did* Van Gogh come into her mind? Could there be any reason? And what did he look like — the real murderer?

To think that he might at that moment be walking the streets of Dublin! Again — she saw him. This time he was standing on Butt Bridge, leaning over the parapet and staring down the river. Another wave of terror swept over her.

'Did you say the other murder was in Dublin too, Don?' she asked sharply.

'Still trying to connect the two? I tell you, there was no connection between them, Mag. This other poor creature —' and he nodded down at the paper — 'this other poor creature was the soul of respectability——'

'— it was a woman too?'

'An elderly spinster,' said Don, as if not altogether corroborating her statement. 'A school-teacher, I think it said.' He bent and looked for verity to the paper. 'Yes, a school-teacher living in Sandford Road. Respectable enough address! Over fifty, too!'

But Mag rushed over and grabbed the paper out of his hand.

'Over fifty? Oh, no, Don! No! Why didn't you tell me? That's terribly sad. I didn't realize. I thought it was another of those ugly businesses. Why didn't you tell me it was so sad? The poor creature!'

Don stared at her.

'What's sadder about it than the girl on the docks?' he asked.

But Mag had got her glasses and was gathering up the pages of the paper. 'Where is the front page? Was there a picture of the poor thing?'

'I don't think so,' said Don. 'There was a picture of that girl, though! She was only seventeen. A lovely-looking girl. Now that was what you might call sad! Oh, I know the sort she was, and all that, but she was so young. She had her whole life ahead of her. There is no knowing but she might somehow have been influenced for good before it was too late. And anyhow,' he said limply, 'the other poor thing' — he shrugged his shoulders, 'she can't have had much of a life. She can't have had much to look forward to in the future. Lived alone, kept herself to herself, an odd sort apparently. Say what you like — it wasn't the same as being seventeen!'

'Oh, stop it, Don. I can't bear it. You don't understand. To come to such an end after a lifetime of service.' Mag was poring over the paper. 'Yes! she was a teacher. To make it worse she was a kindergarten teacher — oh, the poor thing. I can't bear to think of it. The head was battered in — with a stone, they think — and bruises on the neck and back.'

'Not a sex crime, anyway,' said Don.

'Oh, Don, how can you? There's no question of anything like that! She was over fifty! Fifty-four. And several people have already come forward, voluntarily, to testify to her character. She led the most normal, regular . . .'

'Nothing very normal or regular about wandering the streets in the small hours!'

'Oh, you didn't read it properly.' Mag consulted the paper again. 'She was *found* in the small hours, but it was *done* before midnight. They haven't given the pathologist's report yet, but the police put the time between eleven and twelve. She wasn't found earlier because the body was dragged into someone's front garden.'

'Nice for those people!' said Don.

'Oh, Don, how can you joke about it! Do you realize that if she had been left in the street, there might have been a spark of life in her when she was found, although it seems she wouldn't have been found at all until daylight only a couple coming home from a dance happened to step inside the garden gate.'

'Nice for them too!' said Don irrepressibly. 'Sorry, Mag, sorry! I feel as bad as you do about it, but you never take any interest in murders, and to hear you carrying on about these women——'

She pulled him up short.

'Don't speak of them in the same breath!' she said coldly.

But he was looking down at the paper again.

'Oh, look, there's more about it in the late-news column. They're looking for any information that may lead to the recovery of a yellow beret believed to have been worn by the victim earlier in the evening.'

Mag pressed her lips together.

'Poor unfortunate girl! She little thought when she was putting on that beret——'

'It wasn't the girl! It was the other woman.'

'The elderly woman? Are you sure? A yellow beret! It sounds more like what a young girl would wear, surely?'

'The old girl must have fancied herself a bit, it seems.'

'Oh, Don, don't take that tone again, please. I'm certain it was simply a case of some fellow attacking her in the hope that she might have money on her. He probably didn't intend anything more than to stun her, but maybe she screamed, the poor thing, and he got frightened and hit her again to keep her quiet. Maybe he didn't realize he'd killed her at all.'

'Then why did he drag her into that garden?'

'Oh, I forgot about that.'

'You forgot about calling Donny too,' said Don. He had got his hat and coat in the hall and was putting them on.

'Oh, he has plenty of time yet,' said Mag. 'All the same, I'll go right up now and call him before I do anything else.' But at the door she turned back. 'Don't go till I come down,' she said, quite without reason.

Or was it, she thought afterwards, that even then, at the foot of the stairs, a vague uneasiness had already taken possession of her? Had she, all morning, been unconsciously aware of a sort of absolute silence upstairs, different altogether from the merely relative silence when the boy was up there, but asleep? Certainly half-way up the stairs she looked into his room through the banister rail and she was outrageously relieved to see that his bed had been slept in, although he was not in it.

'Oh, you're up?' she cried, talking to him, although she wasn't sure whether he was in the room, behind the door, perhaps, taking down his clothes from the clothes hooks, or in the bathroom — or where? 'Where are you?' she asked, when he wasn't in the room. 'Are you in there, Donny?' she asked, outside the bathroom door. 'Where are you, Donny?' she asked sharply, still addressing herself to him. But when she leaned over the banisters to know if he was downstairs, it was to Don she called. 'Is he down there, Don?'

'Why would he be down here?' Don had come to the foot of the stairs. She thought there was an uneasy note in his voice. He started up the stairs.

'Why are you coming up?' she cried.

Then she must have begun to cry, because Don shouted at her.

'Stop that noise, for God's sake, Mag! The boy probably stayed out last night. But what of it? If I had a pound note for every time I stayed out all night when I was his age! He has you spoiled; that's all! There's some perfectly reasonable explanation for his staying out!'

'But he didn't stay out! Wasn't he in bed when I brought up his hot jar last night?'

'He's gone out somewhere then, I expect,' said Don, 'that's all.'

'Where? And when? I was down early. There wasn't a stir in the house. I didn't hear a stir till I heard you!'

Together they stood stupidly, one above the other, in the middle of the stairs.

'He must have gone out during the night then,' said Don.

'But why? And why didn't he tell us?' said Mag. 'He knows I'm a light sleeper. He knows I never mind being wakened. Many a night, before his other exams, he came into my room and sat on the end of the bed to talk for a while when he couldn't sleep.'

'Well, come downstairs anyway,' said Don, more gently. 'There's no use standing up here in the cold. He hasn't done this before, has he? No! You'd have told me, of course. And he didn't have a sign of drink on him last night, I suppose?'

'Has he ever had?' she flashed.

In spite of anxiety that was creeping over him too, Don was irritated by her righteous tone.

'Look here, Mag,' he said, 'it wouldn't be the end of the world, you know, if he *did* take a drink! we can't expect to keep him off it for ever. Moderation is all we can demand from him at his age.'

But Mag set her face tight.

'I'd never believe it of him,' she said. 'Not Donny!'

'Well, how else are you going to account for his behaviour now?'

'Maybe he thought of something he wanted to find out before the exam. You know Donny! If it was anything important — anything for his exam — he'd think nothing of getting up and dressing again and going out to ask some of his pals about it. Not like other fellows that would be too lazy and would leave it to the morning! Donny would never chance leaving anything to the morning!'

'Yes, but in that case he'd have been back in an hour or so.'

'Unless he stayed talking, wherever he went!'

'He would have telephoned!'

'In the middle of the night?'

They looked at each other dully.

'You don't suppose . . . that he might have met with an accident or something?'

'Funny, I never thought of that,' said Don.

Yet, now, it seemed such an obvious thought.

'Hadn't we better do something?' said Mag.

'Like ring the hospitals?'

He went over to the hall table where the phone stood. There, he hesitated.

'Which hospital ought I to ring? Street accidents are usually brought to Jervis Street Hospital, I think, but I don't suppose they are brought there from all parts of the city. I suppose all the hospitals have casualty wards. I wonder where I ought to try first?' Suddenly his hesitancy left him, and confidently he put out his hand to take up the receiver. 'I know what I'll do, I'll ring the police. That's the thing. They must get reports from all the hospitals.' He turned to her. 'Did he have his name on him, I wonder? Or any form of identification?'

When she didn't answer he looked up. She had gone very white in the face. He put down the phone.

'Don't look like that, Mag,' he said. 'I'm sure he's all right. It was only to reassure you that I was phoning at all. We've got a bit hysterical, if you ask me. I think we should wait a bit longer before doing anything. He'll breeze in here any minute, I bet. Wait till you see. And look here, Mag, let me give you a bit of advice. When he does come back . . .'

But he saw that she was in no condition for taking advice.

'Don't ring the police anyway,' she said.

It was the way she said it, dully and flatly, that made him feel suddenly that whatever had come into her mind to trouble her, was out of all proportion to his own vague fears.

'You're not keeping anything from me, are you?' he asked, sharply.

'Oh no,' she cried. 'It's just that I don't think we ought to draw attention to him in case——'

'—— In case he got himself into some scrape or other, is that it? What scrape could he get into?' he asked, stupidly.

'Oh, I don't know,' she said, 'but it seems a bad

time to draw attention to him — with all this going on. . . .'

It could not have been a more formless reference to what they had been discussing at breakfast, but he got her meaning at once, and his face flushed angrily.

'You can't mean that! You just don't know what you're saying!' he said. 'Your own son!'

'Oh, don't go on that way,' she cried. 'You didn't listen to me. You didn't wait for me to finish.'

But he wasn't listening then, either. He was just staring at her.

'Oh please! Please!' said Mag, wearily. 'I only meant that he might be innocently involved, drawn into something against his will, or even accidentally, and afterwards perhaps been afraid of the consequences. That was all I meant!' Then she looked up at him sharply. 'What did you think I meant?'

In enmity each probed the other's eyes for a fear worse than his own.

'Might I ask one thing?' said Don, bitterly. 'Which of these killings is the one in which you think my son — our son — is involved? Battering in the head of an old woman? Or the other one?'

'You know right well the one I mean!' Mag snapped. 'How could he be involved in the other? Nothing on earth could justify killing that poor old creature.'

Don gave a kind of laugh.

'Well! You women are unbelievable. So you consider the poor girl on the docks was fair game for any kind of treatment! Bad luck if it should end as it did — bad luck for the *man*, that is to say!' He turned away as if in disgust, but the next minute he swung back vindictively. 'Tell me this,' he said. 'Just how did you think that anyone could be innocently implicated in a business like that? Your son, for instance!'

'I don't know,' cried Mag. 'It's not fair to take me

up like that. I didn't say I thought anything of the kind. I was only frightened, that's all. Any woman would be the same. Many a time when we were first married, I waited up for you when you were late coming home, watching the clock, and imagining all kinds of things!'

'About *me*?'

'Oh, you don't understand! What comes into one's mind at a time like this has nothing at all to do with the other person. It doesn't mean one thinks any the less of him. It's as if all the badness of the world, all the badness in *oneself*, rushes into one's mind, and starts up a terrible reasonless fear. I *know* Donny is a good boy. And I know he wouldn't do harm to anyone, but he might have been passing that doorway——'

'Down at the docks, on a dark night — it was raining too, the paper said——'

'Well, how do we know what might have brought him down there? How do we know where he is any night he's out, if it comes to that? He could have been passing that way just at the wrong moment, and maybe seen something. Then, who knows what might have happened!'

'But you forget he came home last night! We saw him!' You went up and said good-night to him like you always do!'

She said nothing for a minute.

'I didn't tell you because it seemed silly, but it wasn't quite like always,' she said then, slowly. 'His light went out as I went up the stairs. He had put it out although he heard me coming. I didn't notice it at the time — well, hardly — I tried not to be a bit hurt — but I thought his eyes might be giving him trouble after so much studying all the week. He put out his hand and took the hot bottle. It wasn't *quite* like always.'

'Oh, you're splitting hairs,' said Don, impatiently.

Yet he seemed to be considering her words. 'I think there's something you ought to get straight in your mind though, Mag,' he said then, slowly, 'even if he were to walk right in the door this minute. You've got the thing wrong. It's just possible that a young fellow like our Donny might on occasion have some truck with a girl like that poor girl that was strangled, without it being necessarily taken that he be mixed up in her murder, but he couldn't be mixed up in her murder without it necessarily being taken that he had some sort of truck with her! Get your mind clear on that!'

Mag's mind, however, had unexpectedly cleared itself not only of that, but of all fear.

'Oh, I'm sure we are being ridiculous,' she cried. 'I'm sure there is some simple explanation.' She put her hand gently on Don's arm. 'If it makes you feel better, dear, go ahead and ring the police, though.' But when he said nothing, she spoke still more gently. 'What do you really think?' she asked.

'I don't know what to think now!' he said, roughly. 'You've succeeded in getting me into a fine state.' He moved over and stood at the window. 'Well, well,' he said. 'They didn't hang him yet anyway; he's coming down the road!'

'Oh thank God. Let me look. Where is he?'

She ran to the window, and then, when she had seen him with her own two eyes, she ran towards the door.

'Mag!' Don's voice was so strident she turned back, but instantly, as their eyes met, they were at one again and could seek counsel from each other.

'What will I say to him?' she asked.

'Let him speak first,' he said, authoritatively.

What they didn't realize, either of them, was that Donny with his smile would speak first to them: his smile that was always so open, and with a peculiar sweetness in it.

'I suppose I'm in for it!' he said. 'Or did you miss me? I thought I'd be back before you were awake.' When they didn't answer, he reddened slightly. 'I meant you to come down and find me as fresh as a lark instead of like most mornings, trying to get my eyes unstuck.' He turned to Mag. 'Were you worried, Mother? I'm sorry. I'll tell you how it happened, but I hope you weren't worried.'

Mag felt flustered.

'Well, it was mostly on account of your exam, Donny —' she said, vaguely, glancing at the pink card. 'If it was an ordinary morning . . .'

Donny glanced at the card too, and also at the clock. He went over and took up the card and put it in his pocket. 'I mustn't forget this. It's a good job I came home. I'd have forgotten it. I wasn't going to come home at all, but go right on to the College, only for thinking about you and how you might worry.'

'It was a bit late in the day to begin worrying about us then,' said Don.

'I know,' cried Donny. 'But I ought to have been home hours ago, only I got a darned blister on my heel. It hurts like hell still. I ought to bathe my foot, but I don't suppose I've time. If it wasn't for knowing you'd have been in a state about me, I could have bathed my foot in the lavatory down at the examination hall. But then I'd have had nothing to eat, and I'm starving.' Seeing some unbuttered toast, he picked it up and rammed it into his mouth.

'Oh, that toast is cold,' cried Mag. 'Let me make some more.'

But Don brought his fist down on the table.

'Toast be damned,' he said. 'Where the hell was he! that's what we want to know. Where were you? You don't seem to realize — your mother was nearly out of her mind.'

'Oh Don, what does it matter now!' cried Mag — 'as long as he's back, and everything is all right.'

For of course, everything was all right now. Only the absent son had been unknowable, capable of — well — anything. The real Donny, standing in their midst, was once more enclosed within the limits of their loving concept of him.

But Don could be so stubborn. 'How are we so sure everything is all right?' he snapped. 'My God, Mag, but you have a short memory!' He turned to Donny. 'It's a queer thing to find a person has got up out of his bed in the middle of the night, and taken himself off somewhere — God knows where — without as much as a word of explanation. Why didn't you tell your mother where you were going? You know she's a light sleeper, and you knew you needn't have been afraid of waking me: I'd never have heard you. Why didn't you do that? Why didn't you tell her what was going on?'

'Oh Don, don't upset him,' cried Mag. 'Look at the clock. He can tell us at supper tonight, and——'

'There's nothing to tell!' cried Donny. 'It'll sound foolish now. It would have been so different if I'd got back before you were awake. I only meant to go out for a few minutes in the first place, but the night was so fine——'

'Are you trying to tell us you just went out for a nice little walk?' said Don. 'In the middle of the night?'

Missing the ironic note in his father's voice, Donny turned round eagerly.

'Not a walk — I didn't even mean to do that! I only intended getting a breath of air.' He turned back to Mag. 'I couldn't sleep after I went to bed. You know how it is before an exam! Well, after I was a while tossing about, I knew I'd never sleep. I knew the state I'd be in for the exam, so I got up and dressed. I thought I'd look over the books again for a bit, but then I thought I'd step

outside the door and get a breath of air first. I had no idea
of going for a walk. That hour of night! I only meant
to stand at the door, or take a few steps down the road.
But it was such a night! You've no idea. I just kept
walking on and on, till I found myself nearly in Goats-
town! I was actually standing on Milltown Bridge before
I realized how far I'd walked! And there were the hills
across from me when I leant over the bridge — and
somehow they seemed so near and——'

'You didn't go up the hills?' cried Mag.

'Well, as far as the Lamb Doyle's,' said Donny. 'I'd
have liked to go on further, up by Ticknock, but it was
beginning to get bright — not that it was really dark at
all, but day was breaking — you should have seen the
sky — I'd like to have stayed up there. But I had the
old exam to think about, so I had to start coming down
again. Oh, but it was great up there; I felt wonderful.
I'd been going a bit hard at the work in the last few
weeks and everything was sort of bunged up in my brain.
Up there, though, I could feel my mind clearing and
everything falling into place. But I don't suppose you
understand?' he said, suddenly aware of their lack of
comment.

'If only you'd come to my door, son,' said Mag.

'As if you'd have let me go, Mother! You know you'd
have got up and come downstairs, and it would be cups
of tea, and re-heating jars and re-making beds. You'd
never have let me out! But that breath of air, and the
exercise, was just what I needed. I felt great! The
good is well taken out of it now though by all this fuss!'
he cried, looking accusingly from one to the other of them.

Mag turned to Don.

'Now! What did I tell you! He could have explained
everything at supper.'

'Let's have no more of it so,' said Don, and he took up
his brief-case. 'All I'll say is, it's a pity he didn't cut

short his capers by an hour or so, and save us all this commotion.'

'I told you I got a blister on my heel,' said Donny, indignantly. 'I would have been back hours ago only for that.'

'Oh! Let me look at it!' cried Mag. 'The dye of your sock might get into it. You could get an infection. We'll have to see that it's clean and put a bit of bandage on it. Sit down, son,' she said, and as he sat down, she sank down on her knees in front of him like when she used to tie his shoe-laces for school.

'Wait till you see the bandage that's on it now,' said Donny. 'I came down part way in my bare feet — as far as Sandyford, where the bungalows begin — but people were stirring, milkmen, bus conductors, and that class of person, going to work, and I had to put on the shoes, but I wouldn't have got far in them only I found something to pad my heel. This!' he cried, and he rolled down his sock and pulled it up — a bit of sweat-stained, blood-soaked yellow felt. 'What's the matter?' he cried, as he saw Mag's face. Then he saw Don's. 'What's the matter?'

Was it the texture of the cloth? Was it the colour? What was it that made them know, instantly, that it had once been part of a woman's beret?

'Why are you staring at me?' he cried. He looked down at the bit of stuff. At the same time he shoved his hand into his pocket and brought up the rest of the beret. 'I felt bad about cutting it up,' he said, 'it looked brand new, but I told myself that somebody's loss was my gain.'

Mag and Don were staring stupidly at him.

'I suppose it wasn't all a yarn you were spinning us, was it?' asked Don at last. But he answered his own question. 'I suppose it wasn't,' he said, dejectedly. And he walked over and took up the paper. 'There's something you'd better know, boy,' he said, quietly. 'You evidently didn't see the morning paper.' He held it out to him, pointing to one paragraph only.

Donny read quickly — a line or two.

'Is this it, do you think?' he asked then, with a dazed look at the bit of yellow felt.

'That's what we want to know,' said Don. 'Where did you get it?'

'I told you! I picked it up in the gutter, somewhere about Sandford Road. Oh, do you think it's it?' he cried again, and letting the pieces fall, he ran his hands down the sides of his trouser legs, over and over again, as if wiping them. 'Why didn't you tell me when I came in first?' he said, looking pathetically young and stupid. But Mag began to laugh with odd gulping laughs.

'Don't mind me, son,' she said, between the gulps. 'I can't help it.' She didn't see the warning look Don gave her. 'It's from relief,' she said.

Donny looked at her. He had not missed his father's look. Ignoring her, he turned to Don.

'What did she mean?'

'Nothing, boy, nothing,' said Don. 'We were a bit alarmed, you must realize that. You wouldn't understand, I suppose. Some day you may. Parenthood isn't easy — it induces all kinds of hysterical states in people at times — men as well as women!' he added, staunchly, taking Mag's arm and linking them together for a minute. 'I mean —' he said, but suddenly irritation got the better of him. 'Anyway you've only yourself to blame,' he snapped. 'We were beside ourselves with anxiety — almost out of our minds. We were ready to think anything.

Donny said nothing for a moment.

'You were ready to think anything!' he repeated, slowly. 'But not anything bad?' He turned to Mag. 'Not you, Mother? You didn't think anything bad about me? Why, you know me all through, Mother, don't you, like — like as if I were made of glass. How could you think anything bad about me?'

'Oh, of course I couldn't,' cried Mag, and she longed to deny everything : words, thoughts, feelings, everything, but all she could do was show contrition — 'I was nearly crazy, Donny,' she cried. 'You don't understand.'

'You're right there ! I don't understand,' said Donny. He slumped down on a chair. After a minute, apathetically he began to pull on his sock over his grimy foot. 'I'd better go to my exam,' he said.

'Your exam !' shouted Don. 'Are you joking ? Well, let me tell you, you can kiss good-bye to your exam. Don't you know you'll have to account for that beret being in your possession, you young fool ? You don't think you can walk into the house with a thing like that — like a dog'd drag in a bone — and when you've dropped it at our feet, walk off unconcerned about your business ?' Suddenly Don, too, slumped down on a chair. 'Oh, weren't you the fool to get us into this mess ! You and your rambles ! If you were safe in your bed where you belonged we'd have been spared all this shame and humiliation.'

'Shame ! Humiliation ?'

Mag thought all that was over at least. Don gave her a withering look.

'We'll be a nice laughing-stock !' he said. 'I can just see them reading about this in the office. There'll be queer guffaws.' He looked at Donny. 'And I'd say your pals in the University will have many a good snigger at you too. To say nothing of what view the University authorities may take of it. And they might be nearer the mark. It's not such a laughing matter at all. It's no joke being implicated in a thing like this. There's no end to the echoes a thing like this could have — all through your life ! People have queer, twisted memories. They'll

never remember that you were innocent : they'll only
remember that you had something to do with it.   I'd
take my oath that from this day you're liable to be pointed
out as the fellow that had something to do with the murder
of a woman.'   In malice he turned to Mag.   'They'll
probably get things mixed up, seeing they were both the
same night, and think it was in the other murder he was
involved !'

Donny didn't catch the last reference.   He was thinking
over what Don had first said.

'God help innocence if everyone is as good at distorting
things as you !' he said, angrily.

'Well, it's no harm for you to be shown what can be
done in that line,' said Don, a bit shamefaced, but still
stubborn.   'I'd be prepared to swear you'll want your
wits about you when you're telling the police about it.
They'll need a lot of convincing before they believe in
your innocence — or your foolishness, as I'd be more inclined to call it — it isn't as if you only saw the thing, or
picked it up and hung it on the spike of a railing, as many
a one would have done — as I'd have done, if it was me !
It isn't even as if you picked it up and put it in your
pocket and forgot about it, as maybe another might have
done.   But oh no !   You had to cut it up in pieces !   How
will *that* appear in the eyes of the police ?   And I must say
I wouldn't like to be you when it comes to telling them
about the blister on your heel ! — As if you were a young
girl with feet as tender as a flower !   Those fellows have
feet of cast iron.   You couldn't blister them with a firing
iron !   I tell you, you'll wear out the tongue in your head
before you'll satisfy those fellows about this.   Oh, how
did it happen to us !'

Mag ran over to him.

'Don !   I can't understand you !' she cried.   'You
didn't take on this bad when we thought —'

Don glared at her.   'It wasn't me thought it, but you,'

he cried. 'And if it was now, I'd know better what to think. He's only a fool — that's clear.'

But Donny stood up.

'I may be a fool,' he said, 'but I'm not one all the way through,' he said quietly, calmly. How is anyone to know — about this? It was hardly light when I picked it up. There wasn't a soul in sight. And if no one knows, why should I go out of my way to tell about it? It was up to the police to find it anyway. Isn't that what they're paid for — paid for by us and people like us? Whose fault is it if they don't do their job properly? There must have been any number of them in that vicinity last night, with flashlights and car lights and the rest of it. If the beret was so important, why didn't they make it their business to find it? Why was it left for me? And why should I neglect my business because they don't do their business right? Here — I'm going out to my exam!'

'Oh, but son,' cried Mag, 'you could call at the station — or phone them — yes, that would be quicker — phone them — and tell them you found the beret, but that you had to go to your exam.'

Donny sneered.

'A lot they'd care about my exam. They'd keep me half the day questioning me, like Dad said.'

'Not if you explained, son. You could say you'd be available in the afternoon.'

'As if they'd wait till then for their information, Mother! And if you think they would be prepared to wait till then, what's the point in my rushing to them now? No — I'm going to the exam.'

'Oh son! Time might be of the greatest importance!' She ran over to him. 'Oh Donny! You don't understand,' cried Mag. 'Even if you were to miss your exam — think of what this might mean — it might lead to their finding whoever did it!'

Don had said nothing for some minutes.

'It could lead them astray as easily,' he said then, very quietly. 'I know them — they could lose more time probing Donny than would find twenty murderers in another country. It might not be as bad as it seemed at first, Mag, for him to do as he says: keep his mouth shut!' He stooped and picked up the two pieces of felt and stared at them.

Donny put out his hand.

'Give them to me anyway,' he said. 'I've got to go.' Almost absently, he fitted the two pieces together for a minute till they made a whole. 'I'll see later what I'll do,' he said. Then he looked Don in the face. 'But I think I know already,' he said.

Hastily, Don took up his brief-case again.

'I'll be down the street with you, son,' he said. 'We have to consider this from every angle.' At the door he turned. 'Are you all right, Mag?' he asked.

Mag wasn't looking at him. She was looking at Donny.

'Don't look at me like that, Mother!' cried Donny. 'Nobody's made of glass, anyway. Nobody!'

The Living

'How many dead people do you know?' said Mickser, suddenly.

Immediately, painfully, I felt my answer would show me once more inferior to him.

'Do you mean ghosts?' I said, slowly, to gain time.

'No,' said Mickser, 'I mean corpses.'

'But don't they get buried?' I cried.

'They're not buried for three days,' said Mickser, scathingly. 'They have to be scrubbed and laid out and waked. You're not allowed to keep them any longer than that, though, because their eyes go like this,' and he put up his hands to his eyes and drew down the lower lids to show the inner lids swimming with watery blood. 'They rot,' he explained, succinctly.

'Mind would you fall!' said I, hastily, thinking he might let go his eyelids if he had to steady himself on the gate-post.

We were sitting one on each pier of the big gate-posts at the school-house that was down on the main road. We were supposed to be sitting there watching the cars coming home from the Carlow and Kerry football finals. But it wasn't much fun. As Mickser said, it was only the family man that came home straight after a match. The real followers, by which he meant the enthusiasts, didn't come home till near night; or near morning, maybe! And they were the only ones it was any sport to watch.

'Those ones have no drink taken,' said Mickser, contemptuously, of the cars that were going past at the time.

'It's great sport when the drunks are coming home,' he said. 'Passing each other out on the roads; on the corners, mind! But your mammy wouldn't let you stay out long enough for that.'

It was only too true. It was a wonder she let me down to the road at all. You'd think she knew there'd be no fun in it. She had a terrible dread of fun, my mammy. She always saw danger in it.

'You can go down to the school-house and look at the cars coming home if you're careful. And mind yourself!' she said to me. 'Keep well in from the road! And wait a minute. Don't sit up on that high wall the way I saw you doing once.'

That was why we were up on the gate-posts, although they were much higher than the wall.

'Gate-posts isn't walls,' said Mickser, definitively.

That was Mickser all over. You could count on him to get you out of anything. But he could get you into anything too! You never knew where a word would lead you with him. This talk about dead people seemed safe enough though.

'How many do you know, Mickser?' I asked, fearful, but fascinated.

'Oh, I couldn't count them,' said Mickser, loftily. 'I bet you don't know any at all.'

'My grandfather's dead.'

'How long is he dead?'

'He died the year I was born,' I said. 'On the very day after,' I added, importantly, having heard it told by my mother to many people.

'Bah!' said Mickser. 'You can't count him. If you could, then you could count your great-grandfather, and your great-great-grandfather, and your great-great-great-grandfather and —' but he stopped enumerating them suddenly as a more vivid denunciation of my foolishness occurred to him. 'Isn't the ground full of dead people that nobody knew.' He pointed down below us to where, through the nettles, the clay under the wall showed black

and sour. 'If you took up a spade this minute,' he said,
'and began digging down there, or anywhere you liked,
you'd be no time digging till you'd come on bones;
somebody's bones! Oh no!' he shook his head; 'you
can't count people you didn't *see* dead, like my Uncle Bat,
that was sitting up eating a boiled egg one minute, and
lying back dead the next minute. He's the best one on
my list though,' he added, magnanimously. 'I saw him
alive *and* dead. But most of them I only saw dead, like
my two aunts that died within a week of each other.
Everyone said it was a pity if they had to go it couldn't
have been closer together so they could have made the
one wake of it. But if they did I might have to count
them as one. What do you think?' He didn't wait for
an answer. 'How many is that?' he asked. 'How many
have I now?'

'Only three,' I said, and my heart rose. He mightn't
be able to think of any more.

Not a chance of it. He looked at me severely. He was
a bit of a mind-reader as well as everything else. 'I want
to pick out the good ones for first,' he said.

That overwhelmed me altogether.

'Ah sure, Mickser,' I said, frankly and fairly, 'you
needn't strain yourself thinking of good ones for me,
because I never saw one at all. One of my aunts died a
year ago all right, and they had to take me to the funeral
because they had no one to leave me with, but they wouldn't
let me into the house till the funeral was ready to move
off. They took it in turns to sit out in the car with me.'

'And what was that for?' said Mickser, looking blankly
at me.

'I don't know,' I said, in a grieved voice, but after a
bit, in fairness to my mother and father, I felt obliged to
hazard a reason for their behaviour. 'Maybe they thought
I'd be dreaming of it in my sleep!

'Not that it did much good keeping me outside,' I

said, 'because I dreamt about it all the same. I kept them up till morning, nightmaring about coffins and hearses!'

'Did you?' said Mickser, genuinely interested, but baffled too, I could see. 'Coffins and hearses,' he reflected. 'What was there about them to have you nightmaring? It's corpses that give people the creeps.' He looked at me with further interest; with curiosity. 'I wonder what way you'd take on if you saw a corpse!' he said. And then suddenly he snapped his fingers together. 'I have it!' he said. 'There's a wake in a cottage the other side of the town.'

'Mind would you fall,' I cried, urgently this time, because there looked to be every danger of it with the way he was hopping about on his pants with excitement.

'Do you know the cottage I mean? It's at the level-crossing. Do you know the woman in it; the one that opens and shuts the railway gates? Well, her son is dead. Did you know that? Did you ever see him?

'A big fellow with red hair is it?'

'That's the one,' he cried. 'She used to have him sitting outside the cottage most days on a chair in the sun. He was a class of delicate,' deftly Mickser tapped his own pate. 'Up here,' he said. 'Did you know that? Well, he's dead now anyway. He died this morning. Isn't it a bit of luck I was put in mind of it?'

'This is your chance of having one corpse, anyway, for your list. But we'd want to get there quick,' he said, taking one jump down off the gate-pier, into the nettles and all without minding them any more than if he was a dog. 'We'll have to get down there before the crowds,' 'They'll be glad to see us no matter who we are, if we're the first to come. They're always glad to see the first signs of people arriving, after the cleaning and scrubbing they've been at all night. And they love to see children above all — at first, that is to say. "Look

who we have here," they say,' he mimicked, in a voice
that nearly made myself fall off the pier. ' "Bless their
little hearts," ' he went on. ' "Come in, child," they
say, and they lead you inside, telling each other that
there's no prayers like the prayers of a child. Up they
bring you straight to the bed, and down they put you
kneeling beside it where you can get a good gawk at
everything. Oh, but it's a different story altogether, I
can tell you, if you leave it till late in the evening. They've
got wise to things very quick, and you haven't a chance
of getting inside the door. " Out of this with you, you
little brats." That's all you'd hear then. "This is no
place for children — out of it, quick!" They'd take the
yard brush to you if you didn't get yourself out of sight
double quick. So we'd better get up there immediately.
What are you waiting for?'

I was hanging back for more reasons than one.

'I was told to stay here,' I said.

'You were told not to be climbing too,' said Mickser,
as quick as a lawyer. 'So you can't say you were doing
what you were told, anyway. Not but that it's doing all
you're told to do, that has you the way you are this day,
knowing nothing about anything. Come on out of that,
and I'll show you a bit of what's going on about you, or if
you don't, I'd dread to think how you'll end up in the
finish. Sure fathers and mothers are the worst people in
the world to depend on for finding out the least thing.
They're all out for keeping us back. I've proved that
many a time with my own ones. And there's yourself!'
he cried. 'To think they wouldn't let you see your own
aunt laid out! I know it wouldn't be me that would be
done out of a thing like that. And what's more, you
oughtn't to put up with it either. You ought to tell them
there'd be no nightmaring or carrying-on about corpses
if you were let get used to them like me. Are you coming,
or are you not?'

It was a sweet, mild afternoon as we set out for the edge of the town to where the level-crossing was, and the small slated house to one side of it. It was very familiar to me when I was a bit smaller and my mother used to take me for a walk out of the town into the country air. We often had to wait for the gates to be opened for us, although the train would have thundered past.

'What is the delay?' my mother would ask impatiently.

'I have to wait for the signals, ma'am,' the woman in charge of them would say. 'You can pass through the wicket gate if you like, ma'am, but that's none of my responsibility.'

'Oh, we're in no hurry,' my mother would say hastily, no doubt to give me good example.

But there was no need. I had heard Mickser say he put a halfpenny on the line one day and the train made a penny out of it. I had no fancy for being flattened out to the size of a man. And anyway, I used to be very curious about the big, white-faced boy that used to be sitting in the little bit of garden outside the house on a chair; a chair brought out of the house, not one you'd leave outside like we had in the garden at home.

'Does she take it in at night?' I asked.

'Of course she does,' said my mother, in a shocked voice, but she must have thought I meant the boy. 'Please don't stare,' she'd say to me. 'Why do I always have to tell you the same thing?'

Only when the gates were opened, and we were crossing over the rails, would she let on to see him for her part. It was always the same.

'How is he today?' she'd ask the woman.

And the woman's answer was always the same too.

'Poorly,' that's what she'd say. At times, but rarely, she'd add few words. 'It's a great cross to me, but I suppose God knows what He's doing.'

'We must hope so anyway,' my mother would say,

hastily, and she'd step over the rails more quickly till we were on the other side. 'How is it,' she said testily to me, 'those gates are always shut no matter what time of the day we want to pass?'

And now here, today, for the first time in my life, the railway gates were wide open.

'Do you think they might have forgot to close them on account of the wake?' I said, hanging back nervously as Mickser dashed over the shining tracks.

He stood in the middle of the line and looked back at me.

'God knows it's high time someone took you in hand,' he said. 'You're nothing but an old babby. What harm would it be if they did forget? Haven't you eyes? Haven't you ears? And if it comes to that, haven't you legs? Come on out of that!' But he slowed down himself and looked up and down the line.

'We're the first here,' he said, when we got to the cottage. 'They're not finished yet,' he said, expertly sizing up the look of the little house.

To me it was like as if it had been washed down from top to bottom like I was washed down myself every Saturday night, and not only the house, but the bit of garden outside it was the same, neatened and tidied, and the big stones that I used to remark around the flower beds keeping back the clay from the grass, were whitewashed every one of them! It was a treat: the stones bright white and the clay bright black with not one weed to be seen out of all the weeds there used to be everywhere. But the chair wasn't out!

'We're too early, maybe,' said Mickser, and he side-stepped suddenly over to the window that was to one side of the door. I couldn't see near so well as him, being behind him, but I saw enough to open my mouth. Between white counterpanes and white tablecloths and white mantlecloths and white doilies, the place was got

up like the chapel at Lady Day. And, in the middle of
it all, like the high altar, was a big bed with a counter-
pane as white and glossy as marble and——

But Mickser didn't let me see any more. He pulled
me away.

'I don't think they're ready yet,' he said. He seemed
to be losing courage just as I was getting mine. He put
his hands in his pockets and sauntered towards the door.

'There now, what did I tell you,' he cried, as we only
missed getting drenched to the skin by a big basin of slops
that was sloshed out the door at that minute.

'Did you ever go down the line?' he asked, suddenly.
And I knew he'd let up altogether on going to the wake.

'I'm not allowed walk on the line,' I said. Anyway,
I was bent on seeing the bed better, and what was on it.
'Let me get a look in the window anyway,' and I skipped
back over the flower-bed, and pasted my face to the glass.

What did I expect to see? I don't know. Not the full-
grown man that was carved out on the bed, hard as stone,
all but his red hair. The hair was real looking, like the
hair on a doll.

'Eh Mickser. Could you give me a leg-up on the
window sill?' I cried, getting more and more curious and
excited.

'Are you pots?' said Mickser. 'If they came out and
caught you up on that window-sill you'd be clouted out
of here with one of those stones,' and he kicked at one of
the big white stones, leaving the black track of his boot on it.

'A true word if ever there was one!' said a voice at
that moment, and a thin bit of a woman in black came
round the gable-end with her sleeves rolled up and no
smile on her, I can tell you. 'Out of here with you!' she
shouted. 'This is no place for you!' Just the very thing
Mickser said wouldn't be said to us.

But before we had time to get out of the flower-bed,
another woman came running out of the front door — the

woman herself that used to have charge of the crossing-gates.

'It's not right to send anyone from the door of a dead-house,' she said, dully.

'Hush now; they're only gossoons,' said the other one.

'He was only a gossoon too,' said our woman. 'Only a child; that was what the priest said to me many a time. Not that he ever had any childhood, any real childhood.' She lost the dull look for a minute; a lively look came into her face. 'Isn't that strange,' she said, 'I never thought of it before, but he was like an old man when he ought to have been a babby; and he was nothing but a babby when he ought to have been a man. I did my best, but it was no use. And you can't do everything, isn't that true? He'd have liked to have other children to keep him company, but they wouldn't understand.'

We weren't sure if it was to us or the other woman she was talking.

I wanted to say that I'd have kept him company, but that I didn't know if my mother would allow me, and as that didn't sound very polite, I said nothing. It was good I did, because I think it was to the other woman she was talking.

'There now! there now!' said the other one. 'Isn't it better God took him before yourself anyway.'

'I used to pray He would,' said the woman, 'but now I'm not so sure. Wasn't it the unnatural thing to have to pray for anyway? Don't all women pray for the opposite; to die before them and not be a burthen on them, and wasn't it a hard thing to have to bring them into the world only to pray for them to be taken out of it. Oh, it's little you know about it, and if there was a woman standing here in front of me, and she had the same story, I'd say the same thing to her. Isn't it little anyone knows about what goes on inside another person?'

She was getting a bit wild looking, and the other woman began dragging at her to get her back into the house. 'Hush now, you'll feel different when time goes on.'

'Will I?' said the mother, looking wonderingly at the other one. 'That's what's said to everyone, but is it true? I'll feel different, maybe, sometimes when I look at the clock and have to pull off my apron and run out to throw back the gates. I'll feel different, maybe, when some woman stops to have a word with me, or when I have to take the jug and go down the road for a sup of milk. But in the middle of the night, or first thing when the jackdaws start talking in the chimney and wake me out of my sleep, will I feel different then? And what if I do forget?' she cried, suddenly pulling her arm free from the other woman. 'I'll have nothing at all then! It will be like as if I never had him at all.' She put her hand up to her head at that and began brushing her hair back from her forehead.

Stepping behind her back, the woman that wanted to be rid of us, started making signs at us to make off with ourselves, but it was too late. The dead man's mother started forward and caught us by the hands.

'We must make the most of every minute we have him,' she cried. 'Come inside and see him. She pushed us in the doorway. 'Kneel down and say a prayer for him,' she commanded, pushing us down on our knees, but her voice was wonderfully gentle now where it had been wild. 'He was never able to pray for himself,' she said, softly, 'but God must listen to the prayers of children if He listens to nothing else. I used to long for him to be able to say one little prayer, and I was always trying to teach him, but he couldn't learn. When he'd be sitting out in the sun on his chair, I used to show him the flowers and tell him God made them. And do you know all he'd say —?' she gave a little laugh before she told us —

' "Who's that fellow?" he'd say! And he'd look round to see if He was behind him! But the priest said God wouldn't heed him; he said he'd make allowances for him. I sometimes think God must have a lot to put up with no more than ourselves. That's why we've no right to complain against Him.'

But I wasn't listening. When she put us kneeling down, I put up my hands to my face and I started to say my prayers, but after a minute or two I opened my fingers and took a look out through them at the man on the bed. I was a bit confused. Why was she saying he was a child? He was a man if ever I saw one! Just then the woman swooped down on me. She saw me looking at him. I thought she might be mad with me, but it was the opposite.

'If only he could see you here now beside him,' she said. She leant across me and began to stroke his hands. And she began to talk to him, instead of about him. 'Here's two nice little boys come to see you!' she said, and then her eyes got very bright and wild again. 'He never had another child come into the house to see him in all his life. He never had another child as much as put out a hand and touch him, isn't that a lonely thing to think?'

It was indeed, I thought. I wonder would it be any use me shaking hands with him now, I thought, and it might be she saw the thought in my eyes.

'Would it be asking too much of you to stroke his hand?' she said, and then, as if she settled it in her own mind that it wouldn't be asking much at all, she got very excited. 'Stand up like good boys,' she said, 'and stroke his hands. Then I won't feel he's going down into his grave so altogether unnatural. No; wait a minute,' she cried, and she got another idea, and she delved her hand into her pocket. 'How would you like to comb his hair?' she cried.

I was nearer to the head of the bed than Mickser, but

Mickser was nearer to her than me, and I couldn't be sure which of us she meant. I wanted above all to be polite, but for that again I didn't want to put myself forward in any way. I stood up in any case so as to be ready if it was me she meant. She was taking a few big red hairs off the comb. Mickser stood up too, but it was only to give me a shove out of his way.

'Let me out of here!' he shouted, and putting the woman and me to either side of him, he bolted for the door. The next minute he was flying across the lines.

And me after him. I told you I wanted to be polite to the people; the dead one included, but after all it was Mickser brought me, and it wouldn't be very polite to him to stay on after him. Not that he showed any appreciation, but he was very white in the face when I caught up with him, and I thought maybe there was something wrong with him.

I was full of talk.

'Well! I have one for my list anyway, now,' I said, cheerfully.

'I suppose you have,' he said, kind of grudgingly I thought, and then he nearly spoiled it all on me. 'That one oughtn't to count by rights,' he said. 'He wasn't all in it when he was alive; he was sort of dead all along!' He tapped his pate again like he did the first time. 'Up here!' he added.

I thought about that for a minute. 'He looked all in it there on the bed!' I said.

But Mickser didn't seem to take well to talking about him at all. 'I've had enough of corpses.'

You don't know how sorry I was to hear that, and I wondering when we'd get a chance to go to another wake.

'You're not done with them altogether, are you, Mickser?'

'I am,' said Mickser, flatly. 'Come on back to the main road. The cars are coming along good-o now.

Can't you hear them? Some of those boyos have a few jars in them, I'd say, in spite of the wives.' He looked expertly into the sky. 'There'll maybe be a fog later on, and in that case they'll all be coming home early; the drunks and all! Come on!'

'Ah, you can go and watch them yourself,' I said. 'I'm going home.'

The truth was I was too excited to sit on any wall for long. I wanted to go home because there were a few things I'd like to find out from mother, if I could bring the talk around to the topic of corpses without letting on where I got the information I had already.

As I ran off from Mickser across the fields for home, I felt that I was a new man. The next time there was a funeral I felt sure there would be no need to leave me sitting out in a car. I felt sure they would all notice a change in me when I went into the house.

'Wipe your feet, son,' my mother cried out to me through the open door of the kitchen, the minute I came in sight. She was often scrubbing the floor. 'Not that you'd be the only one to put tracks all over the place,' she said, and I could see what she meant, because there, in the middle of the floor, was my brother's old bike, up-ended, with the wheels in the air, resting on its saddle, and he busy mending a puncture. Or was it my father she meant? Because he was sitting the other side of the fire with his feet in a basin of water.

It must have been my father she meant, because she lit on him just then. 'This is no place for washing your feet,' she said. 'There's a fire inside in the parlour. Why don't you go in there and wash them? I haven't got room to turn around with you all.'

'The parlour is no place for washing feet,' said my father, quietly, and he pointed to the bike in the middle of the floor. 'When that fellow's done with that bike you'll be glad to have a bit of water on the floor to swish out the mess he'll have made. Why don't you make him take it out in the yard?'

My mother sighed. She was always sighing, but they weren't the kind of sighs you'd heed. They were caused by something we'd done on her, all right, but they were sighs of patience, if you know what I mean, and not complaint.

'It's a bit cold outside,' she said. But she turned to me. 'Here, you, son,' she said, and she picked up my satchel and shoved it under my arm. 'Let you set a good example and go into the parlour and do your homework there by the nice fire.'

But I wasn't going into the empty parlour.

'Dear *knows*! I don't know why I waste my time lighting that fire every day and none of you ever set foot in there until it's nearly night. I only wish I could go in and sit by it. Then I'd leave you the kitchen and welcome.'

But I think she knew well that if she was to go in there that minute, it wouldn't be many minutes more till we'd all be in there along with her, myself and my satchel, and my father with his feet in the basin, and the old bike as well if it could be squeezed in at all between the piano and the chiffonier and all the other big useless pieces of furniture that were kept in there out of the way.

'Ah sure, aren't we all right here,' said my father, 'where we can be looking at you?'

'You must have very little worth looking at if you want to be looking at me,' said my mother, in a sort of voice I knew well that sounded cross but couldn't be, because she always stretched up when she spoke like that, so she'd see into the little mirror on the mantleshelf and she always smiled at what she saw in the glass. And well she might. She always looked pretty, my mother, but she used to look best of all when we were all around her in the kitchen, annoying her and making her cheeks red with the fuss of keeping us in order.

'Mind would you catch your finger in the spokes of that wheel!' she cried just then to my brother.

'Mind would you catch your hair in it, my girl,' said father, because as the kettle boiled and the little kitchen got full of steam, her hair used to loosen and lop around her face like a young girl's. And he caught a hold of her as if to pull her back from the bike.

'Let go of me,' she cried. 'Will you never get sense?'

'I hope not,' said my father, 'and what is more, I don't want you to get too much of it either,' he said.

'Oh, go on with you and your old talk, before the boys and all,' she cried, and then she tried harder to drag herself free.

'She's not as strong as her tongue would have us believe, boys,' said my father, tightening his hold. And then he laughed. 'You'll never be the man I am!' he said, and this time it was my mother herself that giggled, although I didn't see anything specially funny in it.

And that very minute, in the middle of tricking and laughing, my father's face changed and it was like as if he wasn't holding her for fun at all, but the way he'd hold us if he had something against us.

'You're feeling all right these days, aren't you?' he cried. 'You'd tell me if you weren't, wouldn't you?' And then, suddenly, he let her go, and put his hands up to his head. 'Oh, my God, what would I do if anything happened to you!' he said.

'Such talk!' said my mother again, but her voice sounded different too, and although she was free she didn't ask to move away, but stood there beside him, with such a sad look on her face, I suddenly wanted to cry.

And all I had wanted to ask her about the poor fellow at the level crossing came back into my mind. But I didn't feel like asking her then at all. And do you know what came into my mind? It was the words of the prayers we said every night.

ne living and the dead . . .' Over and over
d them, night after night, and I never paid any
But I suddenly felt that they were terrible, ter-
e words, and if we were to be kneeling down at that
moment saying them, I couldn't bear it : I'd start nightmaring, there and then, in the middle of them all, with
the lamps lit, and it not dark.

But the kettle began to spit on the range, and my
mother ran over and lifted it back from the blaze.

'How about us taking our tea in the parlour?' she
cried, 'all of us. The kitchen is no fitter than the back-
yard with you !'

And in the excitement, I forgot all about the living and
the dead. For a long time.

THE END